THE CASE
OF THE
LEFT-HANDED LADY

THE CASE
OF THE
LEFT-HANDED LADY

AN ENOLA HOLMES MYSTERY

NANCY SPRINGER

SLEUTH
PHILOMEL

For my mother

PHILOMEL BOOKS

A division of Penguin Young Readers Group. Published by The Penguin Group.
Penguin Group (USA) Inc., 375 Hudson Street, New York, NY 10014, U.S.A.
Penguin Group (Canada), 90 Eglinton Avenue East, Suite 700, Toronto, Ontario,
Canada M4P 2Y3 (a division of Pearson Penguin Canada Inc.)
Penguin Books Ltd, 80 Strand, London WC2R 0RL, England.
Penguin Ireland, 25 St. Stephen's Green, Dublin 2, Ireland (a division of Penguin Books Ltd.)
Penguin Group (Australia), 250 Camberwell Road, Camberwell, Victoria 3124, Australia
(a division of Pearson Australia Group Pty Ltd).
Penguin Books India Pvt Ltd, 11 Community Centre,
Panchsheel Park, New Delhi - 110 017, India.
Penguin Group (NZ), Cnr Airborne and Rosedale Roads, Albany, Auckland 1310,
New Zealand (a division of Pearson New Zealand Ltd).
Penguin Books (South Africa) (Pty) Ltd, 24 Sturdee Avenue,
Rosebank, Johannesburg 2196, South Africa.
Penguin Books Ltd, Registered Offices: 80 Strand, London WC2R 0RL, England.

Design by Marikka Tamura. The text is set in Cochin.
Library of Congress Cataloging-in-Publication Data
Springer, Nancy. The case of the left-handed lady : an Enola Holmes mystery / Nancy Springer.
p. cm. Summary: Pursued by her much older brother, famed detective Sherlock Holmes,
fourteen-year-old Enola, disguised and using false names, attempts to solve the kidnapping
of a baronet's sixteen-year-old daughter in nineteenth-century London.
[1. Kidnapping—Fiction. 2. Hypnotism—Fiction. 3. Characters in literaure—Fiction.
4. London (England)—History—19th century—Fiction.] 5. Mystery and detective stories.]
I. Title. PZ7.S76846Carl 2007 [Fic]—dc22 2006008261 ISBN 978-0-399-24517-6
1 3 5 7 9 10 8 6 4 2
First Impression

ALSO BY NANCY SPRINGER

THE ENOLA HOLMES MYSTERIES

The Case of the Missing Marquess

THE TALES OF ROWAN HOOD

Rowan Hood, Outlaw Girl of Sherwood Forest
Lionclaw
Outlaw Princess of Sherwood
Wild Boy
Rowan Hood Returns, the Final Chapter

THE TALES FROM CAMELOT

I am Mordred
I am Morgan Le Fay

Ribbiting Tales

London, January, 1889

"WE WOULD NOT BE IN THIS DEPLORABLE situation," declares the younger and taller of the two men in the small club-room, "if you had not tried to bully her into boarding school!" Sharp-featured, and thin to the point of gauntness, pacing the floor in his shining black boots, black trousers, and black cutaway evening jacket with tails, he resembles a black egret.

"My dear brother." Comfortably seated in a deep armchair upholstered in morocco leather, the older, stouter man raises eyebrows like winter hedgerows. "Such bitterness of spirit is not at all in your usual character." He speaks placidly, for this is his club, specifically its very secure private chamber for conversation, and he looks forward to an excellent roast beef dinner as he tells his younger sibling in kindly tones, "While it is undeniable that the foolish girl is on her own in this great cauldron of a city and might already have been robbed and left destitute, or worse, plundered of her virtue—still, you must not allow yourself to become emotionally entangled in the problem."

"How not?" The stalking man swivels to give him a hawklike glare. "She is our sister!"

"And the other missing female is our mother; what of it? Will fretting like a foxhound in a kennel help to find her? If you must blame someone," adds the seated man, folding his hands across the pillowy expanse of his silken waistcoat, "Mother is the person at whom you should direct your ire." Logician that he is, he recites reasons. "It is our mother who let the girl run wild, in knickerbockers, on a bicycle, rather than providing her with instruction in the drawing-room graces. It is our mother who spent her days painting posies while our sister climbed trees, and it is our mother who embezzled the funds that should have gone for governess, dancing-master, decorous feminine dresses, et cetera for the youngster, and it is our mother who ultimately abandoned the girl."

"On the child's fourteenth birthday," mutters the pacing man.

"Birthday or any other day, what does it matter?" complains the older brother, who is beginning to tire of the subject. "Mother is the one who abdicated her responsibility, finally to the point of desertion, and —"

"And then you impose your will upon a broken-hearted young girl, ordering her to leave the only world she has ever known, now trembling beneath her feet —"

"The only rational way to reform her into some semblance of decent young womanhood!" interrupts the older brother with asperity. "You, of all people, should see the logic —"

"Logic is not everything."

"Certainly this is the first time I have ever heard you say so!" No longer placid or comfortable, the stout man sits forward in his armchair, his boots (sheathed by impeccable spats) planted on the parquet floor. He demands, "Why are you so — so over-ridden by emotion, so affected? Why is locating our rebellious runaway sister different than any other little problem —"

"Because she is our sister!"

"So much younger that you have met her exactly twice in your life."

The tall, hawk-faced, restless one actually stands still. "Once would have been enough." His quick, sharp voice has slowed and softened, but he does not look at his brother; rather, he appears to stare through the oak-panelled walls of the club-room to some distant place—or time. He says, "She reminds me of myself when I was that age, all nose and chin, gawky, awkward, simply not fitting in with any—"

"Nonsense!" At once the older brother puts a stop to such balderdash. "Preposterous! She is a *female*. Her intellect is inferior, she requires protection . . . there can be no comparison." Frowning, nevertheless like a statesman he calms his tone in order to take charge. "Such questioning of past events serves no useful purpose; the only rational query now is, how do you propose to find her?"

By an apparent effort of will the tall man reins in his faraway gaze, focusing his keen grey eyes upon his brother. After a pause he says merely, "I have a plan."

"I expect nothing less. Might you share your plan with me?"

Silence.

Settling back into his armchair, the older brother smiles a thin smile. "You needs must have your cloak of mystery, eh, Sherlock?"

The younger brother, also known as the great detective, shrugs his shoulders, his manner now as cold as that of the elder. "There is no useful purpose to be served by telling you anything at this time, my dear Mycroft. If I am in need of your assistance, rest assured I shall call upon you."

"For what purpose have you come here tonight, then?"

"For once, to speak my mind."

"Is it indeed your mind speaking, my dear Sherlock? It seems to me that your mental processes lack discipline. You have allowed your nerves to get the better of you. You seem overwrought."

"A condition preferable, I think, to being not wrought at all." With an air of finality, Sherlock Holmes collects his hat, gloves, and walking stick, then turns towards the door. "Good night, Mycroft."

"My best wishes for the success of your scheme, my dear Sherlock. Good night."

CHAPTER
THE
FIRST

WITH A SHOCK OF ASTONISHMENT I READ the card brought in to me on a silver tray by the page-boy.

"Dr. John Watson, M.D." I spoke the name aloud to assure myself I was seeing it rightly, for I could not believe that this, of all persons, should be the very first client to enter the newly opened—January, 1889—office of London's—and, indeed, the world's—only Scientific Perditorian.

Dr. John Watson? John was a common enough name, but Watson? And a medical doctor? It had to be, but still I did not wish to believe it. "Is it who I think it is, Joddy?"

" 'Ow wud I know, m'lady?"

"Joddy, I have told you before, you are to address me as Miss Meshle. *Miss* Meshle." I rolled my eyes, but what could one expect of a boy whose mother had named him Jodhpur (misspelled Jodper in the parish registry) because riding breeches sounded genteel to her? It was Joddy's awe of my ruffles and puffed sleeves that made him call me "lady," but he mustn't, or people would start asking questions. I wanted the page-boy to retain his awe, which kept him from realising I was actually a mere girl not much older than he, but I wanted him to cease and desist the "m'lady."

More calmly, remembering to guard against any aristocratic edge upon my accent, I asked him, "You have already told the gentleman that Dr. Ragostin is not in?"

"Yes, m'lady. I mean, yes, Miss Meshle."

The Scientific Perditorian's office bore the name of one Dr. Leslie T. Ragostin, because a scientist must needs be a man. But "Dr. Ragostin" would never be in, because he — the Ph.D. kind of doctor — did not exist except in my mind and upon the placards and business cards I placed in shops, kiosks, fruit stalls, and lecture-halls, wherever I could.

"If you would invite Dr. Watson into my office, then, I will see whether I can be of any help."

Joddy ran out, his appearance if not his intellect

smart: all "boy-in-buttons" with braid on his cuffs and down the sides of his trousers, white gloves, striped hat looking rather like a miniature layer cake atop his head—but why not? Most uniforms are absurd.

The moment his back disappeared, I sank into the wooden chair behind my desk, my knees trembling so badly that my silk petticoats rustled. This wouldn't do. Taking a deep breath, I shut my eyes a moment and called to mind my mother's face. Along with that image I could almost hear her voice: "Enola, you will manage very well on your own."

This mental exercise had the desired effect. Calmed, I opened my eyes in time to see Joddy showing Dr. Watson in from the parlour that served as waiting-room.

"Dr. Watson. I am Dr. Ragostin's secretary, Miss Ivy Meshle." Rising and extending my hand to the visitor, I saw exactly what I would expect to see from his writings: a sturdy English gentleman, not well-to-do but definitely of the educated class, with a ruddy face, kind eyes, and a slight inclination towards stoutness.

And I hoped he saw me as I was pretending to be: an utterly conventional young working woman with a bulbous brooch centered upon her dress-front, wearing equally hideous earrings, in general much bedecked in finery of inexpensive materials mimicking the very latest (just as absurd as a uniform) fashion. A girl some of whose fair curls were not her own but had formerly belonged, most likely, to a Bavarian peasant. While respectable, a young female who was not well-bred. One whose father might have been a saddle-maker or a tavern-keeper. A girl most likely preoccupied with pursuit of a husband. If, by means of the aforementioned "brooch" plus a dog-collar necklace, too many ribbons, and the too-obvious hair additions, I had created this impression, then my disguise was successful.

"Pleased to make your acquaintance, Miss Meshle." Dr. Watson had already removed his hat, of course, but quite properly had waited to shake my hand before removing his gloves and entrusting them, along with his walking stick, to the boy.

"Please, sit down." I indicated an armchair. "Do draw close to the hearth. Dreadfully cold out, is it not?"

"Appalling. Never before have I seen the Thames frozen thick enough to skate across." As he spoke, he rubbed his hands together and extended them to the fire. Despite its best efforts, the room was none too warm, and I envied the visitor his cozy upholstered chair. Somehow cold and damp had not troubled me so much before I had come to London, where already I had seen a beggar—or the bodily remains of that person—frozen to the pavement.

Reseating myself on the comfortless wooden chair behind my desk, I hunched my shawl closer around my shoulders, rubbed my own hands (stiff despite the knitted mittens out of which my fingers poked), then picked up my pencil and notepad. "I am so sorry, Dr. Watson, that Dr. Ragostin has gone out. I am sure he would be delighted to meet you. You *are* the same Dr. Watson who is an associate of Mr. Sherlock Holmes, are you not?"

"I am." Polite, indeed humble, he turned to face me as he spoke. "And it is on Mr. Holmes's behalf that I am here."

My heart began pounding so hard, I almost feared my visitor would hear it. No longer could I tell myself some lucky—or unlucky—accident had brought this particular man here.

Here, to consult the world's only professional finder of things, and persons, lost.

But I tried to sound merely polite, with the right

middle-class accent, the right clerical blend of efficiency and servility. "Indeed?" Poised as if to take notes, I asked, "What is the nature of Mr. Holmes's difficulty?"

"I'm sure you will understand, Miss Meshle, that I would prefer to wait and speak privately to Dr. Ragostin."

I smiled. "And I am sure you will understand, Dr. Watson, that I am entrusted to take down the preliminaries, so as to conserve Dr. Ragostin's valuable time. I am Dr. Leslie Ragostin's authorised agent—not to take action, of course," I amended in order to soothe his natural distrust of any female, "but I often serve as his eyes and ears. Just as you do for Mr. Sherlock Holmes," I added, coaxing but trying not to sound as if I were.

Trying not to show how inwardly I begged, *Please. Please, I must know whether I have guessed rightly what brings you here.*

"Um, yes," said Dr. Watson uncertainly. "Quite." He really did have gentle eyes, all the more so when he was worried. "But I am not sure—the matter is delicate—you see, Holmes does not know about this visit."

But—my brother has not sent him?

My heart settled down somewhat, yet began to ache.

Rather dully I told Dr. Watson, "You can rely on my complete discretion."

"Quite. Of course." And as if somehow my diminishing interest had cajoled him, a troubled soul, into unburdening himself to me, he grasped the arms of his chair and began his narration.

"Doubtless you know that I boarded for several years with Mr. Sherlock Holmes at the beginning of his astounding career, but as I am now married and in general practice as a medical doctor, I see far less of him than I did formerly. It has not escaped my notice, however, that since this past summer he has seemed uneasy in his mind, and over the past few months positively distraught, to the extent that he is not eating properly, nor sleeping, and I have become concerned for him not only as a friend but as a physician. He has lost weight, his colour is unhealthy, and he has grown quite melancholy and irritable."

Busily noting down all this for "Dr. Ragostin," I was able to keep my head lowered over my desk so that Dr. Watson would not see my face. A good thing, for I am sure dismay showed; tears formed in my eyes. My brother, paragon of the coldly logical mind, distraught? Unable to eat or sleep? I had no idea that he was capable of such depth of feeling. Least of all about me.

Dr. Watson went on. "Although I have asked him repeatedly what is troubling him so, he denies being in any difficulty, and when yesterday I persisted in questioning him, he flew into such a temper, so out of keeping with his usual steely self-control, indeed so irrational, that I felt I must act upon my concerns whether he liked it or not, for his own sake. Therefore, I sought out his brother, Mr. Mycroft Holmes—"

Ivy Meshle, I realised, should know nothing of Sherlock Holmes's brother. Therefore I interrupted, "How does one spell his name, please?"

"It is an odd name, is it not." Watson spelled it for me, gave me Mycroft's address in London, then continued. "After some hesitation, Mycroft Holmes explained to me that he and Sherlock Holmes have the singular misfortune of being unable to locate their mother. And not only their mother, gone without a trace, but also their younger sister. Two family members—their only remaining family, actually—have vanished."

"How dreadful," I murmured, keeping my eyes down. I no longer felt inclined to weep; instead, I wanted to smile—indeed, I wanted to thumb my nose at my ever-so-eldest brother Mycroft, who had wanted to make a mincing young lady of me—and I found it difficult to maintain a suitably concerned expression as I played the part of one who knew nothing of the matter. "Kidnapped?"

Dr. Watson shook his head. "There have been no ransom demands. No, they are runaways."

"How shocking." I remembered to remain ignorant. "They have gone off together?"

"No! Separately. The mother went missing last summer, and the girl ran away six weeks later, as she was being sent to boarding school. She went alone. I believe that is why Holmes has taken the matter so much to heart. If the girl were with her mother, you see, he might not approve, but he would know his sister was safe. However, it seems that the girl—who is still quite a child—has travelled all by herself to London!"

"A child, you say?"

"A mere fourteen years of age. Mycroft Holmes

told me that he and his brother have reason to believe the girl has access to considerable funds—"

I stiffened, feeling a stab of anxiety, for how on earth could they guess that?

"—and they fear she is disguising herself as a young gentleman of leisure—"

I relaxed, for nothing could be less true. I hoped never to descend to the theatrical cliché of disguising myself as male. Although certainly I did not limit myself to being Ivy Meshle.

"—and as such she might be exposed to decadent influences," Dr. Watson was saying, "and may be trapped into a life of ill repute."

Ill repute? I hadn't the vaguest notion what he was talking about, but dutifully noted it down. "Mr. Mycroft Holmes and Mr. Sherlock Holmes have some reason for thinking this?" I inquired.

"Yes. The mother was, or is, a most determined Suffragist, and the girl herself is of a regrettably unfeminine mould, it would seem."

"Indeed. How sad." Glancing up at him from under a pouf of false bangs, I fluttered my false eyelashes and smiled with subtly tinted lips; indeed, I used a hint of a disreputable substance called "rouge" all over my face to change the sallow, aristocratic

15

tone of my skin to a heartier, more ordinary pink. "Could you provide Dr. Ragostin with a photograph of the girl?"

"No. Nor of the woman, either. It would seem that both avoided photographers."

"What ever for?"

He sighed, his facial expression becoming for the first time somewhat less than kind. "Part of their determination to act contrary to the laws of feminine nature, I suppose."

"Could you give me their names, please, and describe them?"

He spelt the names for me: Lady Eudoria Vernet Holmes, Miss Enola Holmes. (Mum had showed prescience when she named me Enola, which, backwards, spells "alone.")

Dr. Watson said, "From what I have been told, the girl is the more remarkable of the two. Quite tall and thin—"

I had been trying to gain weight, but so far unsuccessfully, due to the fish-head soups and sheep's-head stews served by my thrifty landlady.

"—with a long face, a pronounced, ah, that is to say, rather Ciceronian nose and chin—"

What a very tactful way to say that I looked entirely too much like my brother Sherlock. Having failed yet to make myself plump, I kept inside my mouth, one in each cheek, a pair of rubber devices that were actually intended for filling out another, unmentionable part of the personage. They, along with nostril inserts, quite altered the shape of my face.

"—and an angular personage rather lacking in feminine charm," continued Dr. Watson. "She has shown a preference for masculine clothing and tomboyish activities, walks with a long, masculine stride, and altogether may be entirely lost to decent society if she is not soon found."

"And the mother?" I asked, in order to change the subject before I burst out laughing.

"Sixty-four years of age, but appears considerably younger. Physically unremarkable, but in temperament strong-minded and willful. A talented artist who has unfortunately turned her energies to the cause of women's so-called rights."

"Oh. She wishes to wear trousers?"

He smiled at my apparent scorn for such reformers. "Quite likely. She favors so-called 'rational dress.'"

"And are there any indications at all as to where she might be found?"

"None. But the girl, as I have said, is thought to be in London."

I put down my pencil to face him. "Very well, Dr. Watson, I will inform Dr. Ragostin of the particulars. But I must warn you that he is unlikely to take the case." My very first case, an impossible predicament: to find myself? I could not possibly touch it.

"Why ever not?"

I had already worked out the answer. "Because he does not care to deal with intermediaries. He will ask why Mr. Sherlock Holmes has not come here himself—"

Dr. Watson interrupted with some heat, although his strong feeling was not directed at me. "Because Holmes is too reserved, too proud. If he would not even tell *me* the reason for his distress, do you think he would divulge it to a stranger?"

"But a fellow investigator," I remarked mildly.

"Even worse. He would consider himself humiliated in the presence of—" Rather abruptly Dr. Watson broke off, then asked, "For the matter of that, one must wonder, who *is* this Dr. Ragostin? Begging your pardon, Miss, um . . ."

"Meshle." Take the name *Holmes*, reverse its syllables—*Mes hol*—then spell it the way it is pronounced, *Meshle*; absurdly simple. Yet he would never guess. No one would.

"Miss Meshle. I mean no offense, but I have made inquiries, and nobody has heard of Dr. Ragostin. I came here only because he claims to specialise in finding persons who are lost—"

"Anything that is lost," I interjected.

"But I have found no one who can vouch for him."

"Because he is making his start, just as your friend once had to do. Dr. Ragostin has yet to earn a name for himself. But you will be interested to know that he is a keen student of the methods of Mr. Sherlock Holmes."

"Indeed?" Dr. Watson appeared mollified.

"Yes. He idolises Mr. Holmes, and will be most surprised to hear that his hero has been unable himself to locate his missing mother and sister."

Sitting forward as if his armchair had suddenly become uncomfortable, Dr. Watson cleared his throat. "I suppose," he said slowly, "it might be because Holmes lacks interest in such cases normally. He finds them commonplace and featureless, and generally will not look into them. Why, just yesterday," Watson added, "as I was going in to see

Holmes, out came Sir Eustace Alistair and Lady Alistair, who had been there to beg him to inquire into the whereabouts of their daughter, and he had sent them away with a flea in their ear."

I ignored the logical impossibility of one flea in one ear for two people, because my attention was all taken up by the substance. "Sir Eustace Alistair? His daughter is missing? But I have seen nothing in the newspapers—"

Watson put his fist to his mouth and coughed. "It has been hushed up to prevent scandal."

They feared the girl had gone off with a seducer, then.

I must investigate this matter. I knew that Dr. Watson would tell me no more—already he considered that he had said too much—but he had brought me my first case after all. I would find the missing daughter of the baronet.

Looking none too happy, Watson stood up; the interview was at an end. Reaching for the bell-pull, I rang for Joddy to come see him out.

"I wish to meet Dr. Ragostin personally," Watson told me, "before he takes any action."

"Of course. Your street address? Dr. Ragostin

will be in touch as soon as he has reviewed my notes," I lied.

After I copied the address, I stood to see my visitor out the door.

And after he had left, I seated myself in the armchair he had vacated, by the fire, and rather paradoxically began shivering.

CHAPTER
THE
SECOND

I SHIVERED WITH FEAR.

Of my brother Sherlock, whom I adored.

He was my hero. He was my nemesis. I very nearly worshipped him. But if he tracked me down, I would lose my freedom forever.

Yet—he was distraught on my account?

I could no longer tell myself that I had hurt nothing except his pride.

But what to do? If I gave Sherlock Holmes the slightest hint of my well-being, he would somehow use it to entrap me.

There was Mum to consider, too. How much time did she have left to enjoy freedom and happiness, away from the constraints of propriety and "a woman's place," before she departed this life?

Were men the only ones allowed to have any pride?

My other brother, Mycroft, entered my thoughts only briefly; I did not care whether his pride were hurt. Although quite as intelligent as Sherlock, otherwise he rather resembled last night's left-over cooked potato, cold and inert. He did not care for me enough to try to find me.

But there was another consideration: Why should Mycroft have troubled himself to tell Watson about me?

What if it were all a lie? What if Dr. Watson's visit were a ruse, and Sherlock had himself sent his friend to spy upon me?

Nonsense. My brother couldn't know—

But he somehow *did* know what he should not remotely know, that I had money. And he had perhaps noticed that Dr. Ragostin had taken the offices of the so-called "Astral Perditorian" whom I, Enola Holmes, had helped to send to prison. What if Sherlock Holmes sensed a connection?

Unlikely, I decided after weighing this thought in my mind. More likely, if Sherlock Holmes himself had sent Dr. Watson to spy, it was out of curiosity, to assess whether the "Scientific Perditorian" might afford him competition as a detective.

In which case, might it be untrue that my brother was suffering?

But I could have sworn it was genuine concern I had seen in Dr. Watson's eyes.

Confound it, how was I supposed to know what to do about *family*? Spiritualist levitation seemed less mysterious to me.

I wished I could consult with Mum. However, I had not seen her since the fateful day last July when she had taken her unexpected departure. Indeed, I did not know exactly where she was. I had been in touch with her only through the personal advertising columns of the *Pall Mall Gazette* (her favourite newspaper, cultured yet more progressive than the *Times*), *Modern Womanhood*, the *Journal of Personal Rights*, and a few other publications, using either ciphers or codes. For instance, when I had hypothesised that she was wandering with the Gypsies, I had placed the following:

My Chrysanthemum: The fourth letter of true love, the fourth letter of purity, the first letter of thoughts, the fourth letter of innocence, the first letter of fidelity, the third or fourth letter of departure, and the first letter of the same. Correct? Ivy

The chrysanthemum had become our code word for "Mum," and the message itself referred simply to certain other blossoms as put forth in *The Meanings of Flowers*, a reference book Mum had given me — such symbolism was common knowledge amongst people who exchanged floral greetings. In my personal advertisement, then — a reverse bouquet, so to speak — *true love* stood for the forget-me-not, *purity* stood for the lily, and so on to include pansy, daisy, ivy, sweet pea, and sweet pea again. The fourth letter of *forget-me-not* was *G*, the fourth letter of *lily* was *Y*, et cetera, to spell out *Gypsies*.

Within a week Mum had replied, by a similar code of flowers, "Yes. Where are you?"

And I had answered in like wise, "London."

Such had been the extent of our communication. I very much wanted to see my mum, yet hesitated due to the strength of my feelings towards her, not all of them kind.

Not all of them sure, either. Therefore, I would rather have located her in my own good time and on my own terms.

But now, such upsetting news of Sherlock . . . it was necessary, I decided, to put my own reservations aside.

I wanted to consult with Mum. I *needed* to consult with Mum.

But I must contact her most cautiously.

I waited until I got home, away from Joddy and the other servants.

While I could have lodged in the comfortable upper floors of the Gothic edifice that housed Dr. Ragostin's offices, for caution's sake I did not. Instead, "Dr. Ragostin" rented those rooms to a variety of rather Bohemian lodgers (thus stabilising my finances), while I had found a quite humble room in the East End, where my brother was not likely to look for me—he would not think his sister would ever venture into such slums. In my run-down place of residence, a decrepit house cramped between smut-coloured tenements, I was the only lodger. The landlady, a sweet, elderly widow named Mrs. Tupper, was blessedly deaf, requiring one to shout into a speaking trumpet she held to her ear. Therefore, she could ask me few questions. The only servant was a daily girl-of-all-work whom I never saw. In every regard the situation was ideal for concealment.

Therefore I waited until evening when, safe in my modest bedchamber, comfortably divested of corset, bust enhancer, and the frills, false hair, and facial inserts of Ivy Meshle, I relaxed near the fire in a dressing-gown, with my feet up on a hassock to escape the cold draughts along the floor.

Pulling a candle closer to my side, I began to compose a cipher to Mum.

DOGWOOD FOUR IRIS TWICE THREE VIOLET AND APPLE BLOSSOM HOW MANY?

This message must be, I had decided, different than previous ones and more difficult. How did brother Sherlock know I had money? This worried me greatly. As he knew that much, had he somehow deciphered, and attributed to Mum and me, earlier communications in the "agony columns" of the *Pall Mall Gazette*?

I took what I had written so far and broke it into groups of three letters:

DOG WOO DFO URI RIS TWI CET HRE EVI OLE TAN DAP PLE BLO SSO MHO WMA NY?

I hadn't mentioned Ivy, for caution's sake, but hoped that Mum would nevertheless recognise the cipher as being from me by its code of flowers. *Iris* symbolised a message.

But also—fervidly I hoped Mum would grasp how the code had changed this time—an iris was unique for having three large petals on top and three on the bottom, a dogwood bloom just as unique for having four petals, and a violet and an apple blossom both had five. I had mentioned the violet because it stood for faithfulness. And the apple blossom because sometimes when I was a little girl Mum would cut an apple crosswise to show me the five-pointed star inside, and explain how the apple and its seeds grew from the five-petalled flower.

Having broken up the message, I reversed it:

NY? WMA MHO SSO BLO PLE DAP TAN OLE EVI HRE CET TWI RIS URI DFO WOO DOG

Scowling, I eyed the question mark. It would make the cipher too easy to solve. I replaced it with what Mum would call a "null":

NYX WMA MHO SSO BLO PLE DAP TAN OLE EVI HRE CET TWI RIS URI DFO WOO DOG

There. I imagined Mum would solve this easily, as it was not unlike the first cipher with which she had perplexed me. But this was a mere preliminary to make Mum think about the number five.

I hoped she would then understand that one can take the alphabet and divide it into five parts:

ABCDE
FGHIJ
KLMNO
PQRST
UVWXYZ

And each part has five letters, except the last; but Z is used so seldom that it can be lumped together with Y.

I then wrote my real message to Mum, LON-DON BRIDGE FALLING DOWN URGENT MUST TALK, and enciphered it thus:

L is in the third group or line of letters, and it is the second letter there: 32. *O* is in the third line, fifth letter: 35.

And so on.

323534143534 124324142215 2444
21113232243432 14355334 514322153445
33514445 45113231

I considered running all the numbers together and letting Mum separate the words afterward, but decided against it. She would have enough difficulty with the cipher (third letter second line, or third line second letter?) and decoding the London Bridge reference, meant to tell her where the trouble was and where I wanted to talk with her.

My final draft read: NYX WMA MHO SSO BLO PLE DAP TAN OLE EVI HRE CET TWI RIS URI DFO WOO DOG 323534143534 124324142215 2444 21113232243432 14355334 514322153445 33514445 45113231

This I copied several times for several different periodicals, triple-checking each copy for accuracy before folding both ends towards the centre and affixing the overlapping edge with wax—ordinary white candle-wax, as I had no colourful sealing-wax. After addressing the blank sides of the papers, I set them aside.

Tomorrow I would take them to Fleet Street.

Then, until Mum answered, there would be nothing to do but wait.

I detested waiting.

In regard to the daughter of Sir Eustace Alistair, again I must wait. I could not pursue that matter until tomorrow.

But I had to do *something* before I would be able to sleep.

So, getting up from my cosy seat by the fire, I began to dress. Again. But differently this time. Instead of ladylike underpinnings, I put on flannel unmentionables that warmed me from wrists to ankles. Then an old corset that had once kept a knife thrust from penetrating my person; I laced it only just tightly enough to keep it on, as I wore it not for vanity, but for defense. And also for armament. Where a steel "busk" had once made the corset's front as rigid as a poker, I had substituted a slender five-inch dagger sheathed in the garment's heavily starched linen. This weapon—double-edged, razor-sharp—I could reach through a placket in the bosom of the garment I now put on: a very simple black dress I had sewed for myself in hopes that it would pass as the habit of a nun. I fastened my high collar, ribbed with whalebone to foil cutthroats. Over thick socks I put on my old black boots. Finally, I arranged a black cowl and veil to cover my head and face.

Such was the apparel of my nighttime life.

CHAPTER THE THIRD

SOFTLY I SLIPPED OUT OF MY ROOM. As was her custom, Mrs. Tupper had retired early to her bedchamber, where, even if she were still awake, the dear deaf old soul could not possibly hear my careful tread as I exited. Since I kept my habit hidden in the bedstead, I felt quite certain Mrs. Tupper had no idea that a second person, so to speak, a rather gaunt, nocturnal Sister of Charity, was lodging in her spare room along with that nice young secretary girl Miss Meshle.

I had to feel my way down the dark stairs, for of course in this sorry house, nearly a hovel, there was no gas laid on. Fumbling for the keyhole in the dark, I unlocked the front door with my latch-key, stepped outside, relocked the door behind me, then walked quickly away to lessen the likelihood that any chance midnight watcher should discover where I lived.

At random, taking a different route than last night or the night before, I strode down shadowy, narrow "courts" ill-lit by gas street-lamps. Not for the East End were the carriage lamps and flambeaux of the well-to-do, nor the brand-new electric fixtures of the very rich. Here, the feeble and wavering lights floated, or rather drowned, in a sea of brown smut; London crouched frigid in its own peculiar, choking way. Here, midnight's chill was made of chimney soot, coal fumes, wood smoke, and dank disease wafting up from the Thames; it was as if one swam in a fog colder than ice yet never frozen, forever soaking through one's clothing and into one's bones. Such thick and freezing weather had driven indoors all folk who had anywhere to take refuge. Even on the stairways of the lodging-houses one would find vagabonds sleeping. Poor folk who had no other fuel tonight were burning straw stolen from dung-heaps behind stables, and might not live to see morning.

When I judged I had left my own lodgings far enough behind, I stepped into a dark gap between houses and lit an oil lantern I had brought with me. Already stiffening with cold, my fingers could barely manipulate the match.

One might well wonder why a young lady of gentle breeding would go out under such circumstances. I myself did not fully understand why I felt compelled to wander the night. I am perhaps a bit of a monomaniac, driven always to quest, venture, search, seek, find. Find out, find things, find people—tonight, anyone who might need help to survive.

Into my habit, as well as the heavy wool mantle I wore over it, I had sewed many deep pockets, stocked with items I might need: candle stubs and wooden matches, shillings and pence, warm knitted socks and caps and mittens, apples, biscuits, a flask of brandy. I carried a homemade blanket over one arm. In the other hand I lifted the lantern.

Wearing black fur-lined gloves, I held my light high and began to search the back ways and byways, alert for any hint of danger, any sounds of angry altercation, or screaming, or footsteps behind me.

I listened also for the sound of anyone crying.

And before very long I heard it.

A low, dull sort of sobbing. Reflexive, as if the person had given up, weeping only to breathe. Guided by that lament—for my lantern showed me only a few paces of street-stone underfoot before all vanished into sooty fog—I found an old woman crouched in a doorway, trying to warm herself in a shawl that covered only her head and shoulders.

As I approached, as she heard my footsteps, she tried to muffle her weeping with her hands, afraid—but then she sobbed aloud again, this time in relief, recognising me. Many such folk knew me by now. "Sister," she whispered, "Sister of the Streets." One thin arm faltered towards me.

Mutely, for the Sister never spoke or made a sound, I swept down on her like—like a big skinny black hen on a chick, I suppose, wrapping her in the blanket I had brought along. A crude thing: I made my blankets out of hunks of old cloth sewn together, because any coverings of better quality would have been stolen from those who needed them most.

This woman's face, lifted to the lantern light, was perhaps not elderly after all, only harrowed by hardship, her scrawny body stunted by rickets and hunger. Was she a widow or a spinster, turned away from a common lodging-house for lack of eight-pence, or had she been driven into the night by a husband's drunken blows? Knowing that I would never know, I slipped thick, knitted stockings over her bare feet, then brought out of one of my pockets an item I had, I believe, invented: a sizable tin tightly stuffed to the brim with wadded paper into which I had poured paraffin. Lighting a wooden match, I laid it atop this odd sort of portable fire and set it in the doorway beside her, where it started to burn, flaring, like an overlarge candle, putting off a good deal of heat. It would last only an hour or so, but long enough for her to warm herself.

And hidden enough, I hoped, so that it would not attract any unwelcome company to her.

I gave her an apple, some biscuits, and a meat pie that had come from a baker, not a street vendor, and therefore might be made of good wholesome meat not intermixed with dog or cat.

"Thank you so much, Sister." The woman could not seem to stop weeping, but she would, I thought, after I went away. Quickly I slipped her a few shillings, money enough to buy her food and lodging for several days, but not so much that she was likely to be killed for it. Then, standing back, I turned away, hoping she understood that there was nothing more I could do for her.

"Sister of the Streets, God bless you!" she called after me.

Her gratitude made me feel like a fraud, a farce, unworthy, for there were many, too many like her, and I could never possibly find them all.

Striding on my way, I myself shivered with cold. And with fear. Listening.

Tipsy singing and drunken yells floated faintly to my ears from the next street. A public house, still open? I wondered how this was allowed. Surely the authorities—

My attention diverted, too late I sensed a presence behind me.

Some small sound, perhaps the chuff of shoe leather against the frozen mud and crushed stone of the street, perhaps the hiss of an evil breath—but even as I opened my startled mouth to gasp, even as I leapt to turn, something seized me around the neck.

Something unseen, behind me.

Fearsomely strong.

Gripping tight, tighter.

Not a human grasp. Some—some narrow doom, serpentine, constricting, biting into my throat—I could not think, and never even reached for my dagger; I only reacted, dropping my lantern as both my hands flew up to claw at the—thing, whatever it was, tormenting my neck—but already I felt my breathing cut off, my body thrashing in pain, my mouth stretching in a voiceless scream, my vision dimming to darkness, and I knew I was going to die.

It seems to me that I next grew aware of a light in the darkness—but not a kindly light; this was orange, dancing, diabolical. Blinking my way out of blackness, I felt the cold harsh street beneath me, and saw that I lay nearly in a fire. A pool of oil, leaking from my broken lantern, burned merrily. In that gleeful glow, three or four men peered down at me—very blurred, that memory. Blurred by night and fog, by my confusion and pain, by my veil. As blurred as their drunken voices.

"Is she dead?"

"What sort o' cad wud garrote the Sister?"

"Mebbe one o' them foreign Anarchists 'oo don't like religion."

"Did any of yer see 'im?"

"Is she breathin'?"

Bending over me, one of them lifted my veil.

I think he looked at my face for a moment before I struck his hands away. Before my shock at such impropriety roused me from my — swoon? No, one can hardly say I had tumbled down in a faint, not in any delicate-lady sense of the word. Surely if one is strangled half dead, one cannot be accused of fainting.

In any event, blinking my way out of unconsciousness took a moment or two, which I remember imperfectly. I believe I struck out at the man who was lifting my veil, yanking it back down over my face again as I rolled away from the fire and wavered to my feet.

" 'Ere, missus, wot's yer 'urry?"

"Steady on, old 'orse."

"Watchit, Sister, ye'll fall."

Hands reached towards me. But rejecting their offers of help — for they were staggering drunk, whereas I was merely staggering — I fled.

I retreated, as the military would say, in bad order. Without ever having drawn a weapon. In a panic of dry sobbing. Indeed I hardly know how I blundered my way back to my lodging. But somehow, eventually, I reached my room, where, trembling, I lit every oil lamp, every candle, and stirred up the hearth fire, wastefully throwing on wood and coal until I'd roused a blaze of warmth and light in the night.

I threw myself into my armchair and sat trying to stop panting, for each breath hurt my throat. Closing my mouth, I swallowed again and again, trying to swallow my humiliation as well as my pain.

Despite the fire, I still felt cold with more than just night's frost, chilled to the marrow of my soul. I needed to get into bed. Staggering up, I began to unbutton my high collar—

My trembling fingers felt something hanging around my neck.

Some alien presence, long and smooth, supple— it was as if a snake clung there. Despite the pain to my injured throat, I cried out as I snatched and clawed at the thing, fumbling it off of me and flinging it to the floor.

There on my hearth-rug it lay.

The garrote.

I had heard that they were made of wire, but this one was fashioned instead of some sort of smooth, white cord knotted to a stick of wood.

Caught in that knot I saw a cluster of brown hair—my own. Wrenched from my head as the garroter had twisted the device tighter and tighter around my neck.

Swaying where I stood, I had to close my eyes for a moment, realising that only my high collar, stiffened with whalebone, had kept me alive. London's constables wore high-collared tunics for the same reason. How astonishing, and fearsome, to think that such a simple device could terrorise an entire metropolis, even the police.

Fearsome also, and shameful, to realise that not any courage or wit of my own had saved me. Forgetting my weapon, like a bumbling fool I had kicked and clawed, no better than any other preyed-upon female. Collar or no collar, I might be dead had those drunkards not happened along. Yes, I decided, indeed, they must have interrupted the garroter. Why else would he have left his lovingly fashioned apparatus around my neck?

Trembling badly, I forced myself to open my eyes again, studying that loathsome device.

Lovingly fashioned, indeed. The stick, of polished malacca wood, might have been taken from a gentleman's cane. Hardly the sort of implement one would expect of a street thug. And the cord —

A stay-lacing.

That is to say, the lacing from a lady's *corset*.

Sudden sickness lurched through me, and with it, a blaze of anger. Snatching up the foul-minded, insolent thing, I flung it into the fire.

CHAPTER THE FOURTH

FOR TWO DAYS I STAYED IN BED, CONVEYING to Mrs. Tupper by signs, as I could barely speak, that I had a sore throat—a common enough ailment at the time of year; I am sure she thought nothing more of it. The high ruffled collar of my nightgown hid my bruised neck.

It could not, however, comfort my bruised and ruffled feelings. While accustomed to physical pain—often enough as a child I had fallen from a bicycle, a horse, a tree—I found myself not at all accustomed to being hurt by another human being in such an offhanded way. It was not only my sore throat that prevented me from eating the soups and jellies Mrs. Tupper offered me. It was the malice of what had happened that made me sick.

Malice, and impropriety—no, far more than impropriety. Some—some *evil* I could not yet name.

Something about the stay-lacing.

What sort of man would attack a woman with a weapon derived from a cane—the sort of stick used to thrash schoolchildren—and a *corset*? Intimate feminine apparel by which upper-class females were compressed to fit into their ridiculous dresses, making them ornamental to society, prone to fainting spells, and susceptible to internal injuries and death? It was largely in order to escape strait-lacing that I had given brothers Mycroft and Sherlock the slip. I had fled so that no so-called boarding school could thrash *me* or try to cut me in half at the waist, and now someone had put that—that thing—around my *neck?*

For what purpose? To rob me of what?

And why with such a strangely disturbing weapon?

Was it indeed a *man* who had attacked me, or some madwoman?

These were questions for which I lacked answers.

By the third day I could talk a little, and I returned to Dr. Ragostin's office, where I made myself comfortable—in body, if not in mind—reading the stack of newspapers that had accumulated during my absence.

I found my message to Mum in the newspapers, for I had sent copies to Fleet Street by post, but I found no message from Mum to me.

Of course it was too early to expect a reply. Still, I could not help looking. I wanted—

This would not do. Feeling sorry for myself like a child, wanting Mummy. What would Mother have told me if she were here? Utterly predictable: "You will do very well on your own, Enola."

A statement I had always accepted as rather a compliment.

But on this particular day, with the pain in my throat exacerbated by a lump that had arisen therein, I suddenly, achingly realised that I wanted—I wanted something. Or someone.

I wanted no longer to be alone.

Enola, alone, with no one to walk by my side.

With no one to confide in.

With no one to comfort me.

Yet I knew quite well that any companionship simply could not be, not for another seven years—

for until I became legally adult, every person who knew me posed a threat to me, of discovery. Joddy, a danger if he learned too much. Mrs. Tupper, likewise. The grocers and bakers who supplied the food I gave to the poor, the washerwoman who did my oddly assorted laundry, the whitesmith who had made my daggers for me, each a risk. I had thought of keeping a pet, but even a dog could ruin me just by recognising me at the wrong time. Old Reginald, the collie from Ferndell, if he were somehow transported to London and encountered me, would hurl himself at me with ecstatic canine cries, no matter how I might be disguised. And if Lane the butler were with him, and Mrs. Lane, if they found me, she would burst into happy tears, for she had been like a mother to me, more so than—

Stop. Enola Holmes, you stop snivelling this instant.

I needed to get up, get moving, accomplish something.

Very well. There was nothing I could do concerning Mum, or concerning Sherlock's distress until I had heard from Mum. And—although I fervidly wished for justice, or, indeed, revenge!—at this point there was nothing I could do about the unknown garroter who had distressed *me*.

But there *was*, surely, something I could do concerning my life's calling: being a perditorian. Something I could do about Sir Eustace Alistair's missing daughter. I had promised myself that, for "his" first case, "Dr. Ragostin" would find her.

I needed to know the particulars.

After some thought, I rose and made my way back through various passageways to the kitchen, where the cook and the housekeeper were having their mid-morning cup of tea. Both looked startled to see me enter that room, and apprehensive, because normally I would have simply rung for service, so what was wrong?

"Mrs. Bailey," I croaked to the cook, "I do not feel quite well. My throat is most dreadfully sore. Do you suppose—"

"Of course," cried Mrs. Bailey, relieved, answering my request before I could frame it. Illness, you see, explained my presence in the kitchen, which due to hearth, stove, and water-heater was by far the warmest place in the house. "Tea?" She jumped up to put the kettle on.

"The very thing. Thank you kindly."

"Do sit down, Miss Meshle," invited the other

one, Mrs. Fitzsimmons, the housekeeper, offering me the chair closest to the fire.

At the table with the two of them, I sipped, briefly answering their inquiries about my health, after which they resumed their conversation. Mrs. Bailey had been to a music-hall the night before to see a Mesmerist, or magnetiser, "one of them pursy, swarthy, shaggy-browed Frenchmen with wolf eyes." He had been assisted by "a wench in one of them French clinging gowns" who lay on an examining-couch while he had her stare at the usual shiny object—in this case, a candle-flame—and flicked his hands at her face as if sprinkling her with his "vital principle," then made the customary magnetic passes over her entire person. "Scandalous close to 'er 'is 'ands come, but 'ee didn't touch her. She lay wit 'er eyes open like a corpse, an' 'ee told 'er to eat soap an' she chewed it down like it was toffee. 'Ee told 'er she were a pony an' she whinnied. 'Ee told her she were a bridge, picked 'er up an' put 'er down again across two chairs and there she lay stiff like stone. 'Ee fired a pistol near her ear . . ."

Sitting and listening, I concealed my impatience with difficulty, for it was all jugglery and rot, of course; Mesmerism had been discredited years ago, along with dead bodies electrically "galvanised" into the appearance of life, incorporeal table-turning, spiritualist slate-writing and all sorts of nonsense masquerading as science and progress.

". . . invited us to come up and test the trance. One gent pinched 'er, and 'is wife passed smelling salts under 'er nose, and me, I run a 'atpin into her an' she never so much as twitched. Then after we was done the Mesmerist made more of them magnetic passes with his hands, and up she jumps, all smiling, an' we give 'em both a real big clap of our 'ands as they went out. Then, the next thing, there was a Phrenologist—"

Oh, no. More pseudo-scientific dust of the past.

I interrupted. "Is it true," I asked, "that the Queen once shaved her head for a Phrenological reading?"

They could scarcely believe it (no wonder, as I had just made it up, thereby, I am sure, spawning a rumour) but anything was possible: Lady This and Lady That had held séances, Duke So-and-so somnambulated, several young Honourable Lords had experimented with laughing gas, et cetera. I had succeeded in changing the subject to the fascinating foibles of the upper classes—about which, like most domestics, these two knew everything. Scandal might be "hushed up" in the newspapers, but no event in any London household was secret so long as there were servants to whisper with other people's maids and footmen. Accepting a second cup of tea, I waited for my opportunity. It came when a member of the peerage was mentioned.

Coughing for attention and sympathy, I asked, "Would he be acquainted with Sir Eustace Alistair?"

" 'Im? I doubt it!" declared Mrs. Fitzsimmons.

"Sir Eustace is just a baronet, don't ye know," said the cook.

"And disgraced, to boot," said the housekeeper with a hushed voice and zestful eyes.

I reacted with satisfactory shock and interest. "Disgraced? How so?"

"By 'is daughter, Lady Cecily! Shameful affair."

" 'Orrendous for 'er parents," said the cook. "One 'ears Lady Alistair is quite prostrated, she is."

The housekeeper replied, the cook interjected, and during the next several minutes between the two of them the story took form, in my mind at least, like a structure emerging from a fog:

The Honourable Lady Cecily Alistair, Sir Eustace's second oldest, just sixteen years of age and not yet presented at court, had gone missing Tuesday of last week, on which morning a ladder had been found at her bedroom window. Upon being questioned by police authorities, girl-friends of Lady Cecily admitted to her having been approached last summer, while in their company ("'ardly never no chaperones anymore, and them girls 'orseback riding, bicycle riding, shopping on their own, wot's the world coming to?") by a young "gent," that is to say, a man of dandified attire but doubtful pedigree. Further inquiry and a search of Lady Cecily's desk revealed that she and the young man had been corresponding, quite without a proper introduction or the knowledge of her parents. It had taken the police, who had only a first name to work with, four days to locate this impertinent male, who had turned out to be a mere shopkeeper's son with no proper sense of his place, very likely with aspirations above his station in life; by then, of course, it was Far Too Late (" 'orrible if she married 'im, an' even worse if she didn't"). But as it turned out, she had not been found with him. The young man had protested in the strongest terms his innocence of any wrongdoing. ("Rubbish. Men wants only one thing.") He had been watched and followed since, but no sign of Lady Cecily had been discovered.

"More tea, Miss Meshle?"

I smiled and shook my head. "No, Mrs. Bailey, thank you very much. I think — I believe I must go attend to business now."

Returning to the front of the establishment, I withdrew from my own outer office into Dr. Ragostin's, instructing Joddy that I was on no account to be disturbed. I often napped in Dr. Ragostin's office during the days, after I had been out all night as the Sister. Judging by Joddy's impertinent grin, which I ignored, he thought I intended to spend a few hours swaddled in "Afghans" on Dr. Ragostin's comfortable chintz sofa.

This was what I wished him and the other servants to think.

Aside from the aforementioned sofa facing the hearth, Dr. Ragostin's inner sanctum featured a rather grandiose desk I had provided for that fictitious personage, leather armchairs for his clients, and the resplendent Turkish carpet upon which those furnishings stood. Between heavily draped windows stood a tall bookshelf, and other bookshelves lined the three remaining walls entirely, except of course that gas sconces upon long mirrors (to reflect the light) separated them. Such plenitude of bookshelves had been left behind by the previous occupant—a so-called spiritualist medium. This had been the séance room.

After locking its door from the inside, closing the thick serge drapes for privacy, and turning up the gas-jet chandelier to illuminate the resulting gloom, I walked to the first bookshelf on the inner wall. There I reached behind a stout volume of Pope's essays, released a silent latch, then pulled the left edge of the bookshelf towards me. With only fingertip pressure, and utterly without sound—for the hinges were perfectly hung and lavishly oiled—the entire shelf swung open like a door to reveal a small room behind it.

Here, I felt sure, the medium's accomplices had hidden.

I, however, used the closet-sized space to hide items of another sort.

Which I now needed. In order to be received at the baronet's residence, I could not go as Ivy Meshle. I needed to effect a transformation.

I lit a candle. Then, shivering with cold—for

54

there was no fire laid on in this room — I pulled off Ivy Meshle's cheap flounced-poplin dress, along with the bulbous brooch she always wore — with a purpose. Welded to my dagger hilt, this brooch looked like an ornament pinned to my dress-front, but actually allowed my weapon's handle to protrude between my buttons. Grasping the "brooch," I drew the dagger from my corset with a flourish, admiring its shining, thin, razor-edged blade a moment before laying it aside.

I laid aside also Ivy Meshle's false hair, earbobs, et cetera, until I stood in my underpinnings, the most essential of which, ironically, was my corset.

Yes, despite my opinion of corsets, I wore one always — but as my protective friend, never tightened to become my tormentor. For me, a corset provided not constraint, but the freedom it gave by furnishing defense, disguise, and supplies. Aside from sheathing my dagger, the corset supported my Bust Enhancer (where I concealed many useful items, including a small fortune in Bank of England notes) by which, along with Hip Regulators, I maintained a figure quite different than that of the unembellished Enola Holmes.

Undressed, then, except for padding, protection,

and petticoats, I bent to a basin and washed away my rouge, grimacing, for the water I kept in the closet was all but freezing, then looked at a mirror. My own long, plain, sallow face, framed by my own long, plain brownish hair, looked back at me.

The hair was a problem. In order to pass as a woman, you see, I had to wear it up. Girls wore their frocks short and their hair long, but women had to wear their dresses long and their hair "up." While almost every other inch of a gentlewoman must be covered during the daytime, her ears, it seemed, must be always bared.

Today I needed to pass as a gentlewoman. Such ladies, however, had maids to arrange their hair for them, and I had none.

I will spare the gentle reader the details of the struggle. Suffice it to say that nearly an hour later a gentlewoman with her hair up—and mostly hidden beneath a formidable hat—emerged from behind a bookshelf. I wore a grey day-dress custom-made of the finest worsted, yet discreet, almost dowdy, in its styling. And yes, with a brooch centered upon its bosom—this time a tasteful oval made of mother-of-pearl. I possessed, you see, more than one dagger.

I put on quite a lovely fur cloak, with a dainty little muff to match, before closing—and concealing—my "dressing-room." Then, approaching a different bookcase, the one that stood by the outer wall, I reached behind another stout tome *(Pilgrim's Progress)*, manipulated another hidden latch, and slipped out of Dr. Ragostin's office by the secret door.

CHAPTER THE FIFTH

MY CRAFTY PREDECESSOR HAD PLACED THIS exit well. I emerged behind a bushy evergreen that grew in the narrow space between houses. From there, I was able to make my way to the street satisfied that no one could possibly have seen me leave, not even that sharp-eyed Mrs. Fitzsimmons, who had probably verbally dissected me with Mrs. Bailey the moment my back was turned: *Poor dear, with more'n enough nose and chin but barely anything else, a woman can tell; if any man ever marries 'er ee'll find 'imself sorely deceived.*

Dealing with my miserable hair—the colour of bog mud, and as limp as the rotting vegetation thereof—had put me in a bad humour. Once safely in a four-wheeler cab, I pulled paper and pencil from one of my pockets and drew a quick, rather rude sketch of Mrs. Fitzsimmons and Mrs. Bailey with their old-fashioned white ruffled house-caps bent together in gossip, their shrewd baggy eyes, their lipless gabbling mouths—rather like a pair of turtles, actually.

Then, having got temper out of the way, I more calmly sketched a picture of a young gentlewoman in a fur cloak and muff and a brimmed velvet hat trimmed with grebe feathers. Beneath this elegant headgear she peered nearsightedly, for no lady, however faulty her vision, will wear glasses. So gently reared as to be nearly helpless, she walked with her head bent and her shoulders drawn in, very plain despite her fine clothing.

Dr. Ragostin's shy child bride, Mrs. Ragostin.

By drawing this, I reminded myself who I was being today.

When the urge to sketch seized me, I could have drawn Ivy Meshle if I wanted to, or Mum, or Sherlock or Mycroft, or just about anyone I knew except Enola Holmes. My true self I could not quite capture on paper. Odd.

The cab took me to a fashionable street. As it pulled to a halt, I stowed my papers deep in a pocket; on two occasions Sherlock Holmes had seen my drawings, and I must be careful never to give myself away by leaving any behind. When I returned to my lodgings, I would burn the sketches.

Alighting at the corner, with both silk-gloved hands tucked into my muff I waited until the cab had driven away. You see, while only dowagers wore bustles anymore—mercy be thanked, their clumsy bulk was going out of fashion—still, a gentlewoman must trail a train. The hem of my long cloak and back of my even longer skirt dragged upon the icy cobbles, indicating the social class of one who rode in carriages. So I stood where I was until the cab had departed. Dr. Ragostin, I knew, really ought to keep his own little brougham and pair, but there were limits, however generous, to the funds Mum had provided me.

Fortunately, I seldom needed be Mrs. Ragostin.

Very fortunately, as I wore my own unaltered face for this purpose. Ivy Meshle could hide behind rouge, fair-hued hair additions, and cheap baubles, but no lady could do so.

As I stood on the corner, two top-hatted gentlemen strode past me with glares of disapproval. "*My* wife stays at home where she belongs, none of this peripatetic nonsense," grumbled one to his companion. "That young lady will bring trouble on herself, wandering about alone," the other agreed, "and 'twill be her own fault." I ignored them, and tried not to let their comments darken the day, which was quite gloomy enough already; although the clocks had just struck one in the afternoon, a lamplighter climbed his ladder, for with the London sky thick with smoke, fog, and soot it might as well have been evening. All over the rooftops of the city, chimneys stood like dark candles spewing smut. Workmen and cleaning-women walked past me coughing; someone would die of the catarrh today.

A ragged little girl with a broom approached me; at my nod the child hurried to sweep the crossing for me, banishing from my path the muck of soot, stone dust, mud, and horse droppings that always coated the street.

Following the child to the other side, I tipped her generously—a penny, not just a farthing—then, myself willy-nilly "sweeping" the pavement with my train, I progressed towards my destination: the residence of Sir Eustace Alistair.

Upon the massive front door I found a large

brass knocker in the shape of a lion's head. Remembering to strike timidly, as befit Mrs. Ragostin, I employed it.

Presently the door was opened by a maid all shining in afternoon black, behind whom stood an equally resplendent butler.

"Her ladyship is not receiving visitors," the butler told me, his manner as cold as the winter day.

"Her ladyship is not feeling well? If you would just take up this card, and my sympathies," I said in the voice of an exceedingly well-bred mouse.

Balefully he fetched his silver tray, upon which I laid the card of Dr. Leslie T. Ragostin, Scientific Perditorian, on which I had penned "Mrs."

"I sent the carriage away," I murmured. "One must be discreet." This to explain the absence of a footman or any other accompanying servant. Stepping inside, for they could hardly leave such a well-dressed lady freezing upon the doorstep, I added, "I will just warm myself by the fire."

The maid was good enough to take my cloak and muff—not my hat; a lady's hat and hair, once arranged, remained inseparable. Hatted and gloved indoors, I could not have looked more absurdly upper-class.

Still, loitering in the rather grand parlour, I had no idea whether Lady Theodora—that was the wife's name, Theodora; I had looked up "Alistair, Sir Eustace, Baronet" in Dr. Ragostin's copy of *Boyles* to find the address—as I say, I did not know whether the lady would condescend to see me. She might find my unexpected arrival a straw worth grasping at. On the other hand, depending on whether pride outweighed desperation, she might consider such presumption to be the last straw.

Trying to imagine the dialogue taking place upstairs, I could only hope the lady understood what *perditorian* meant, and that the butler had been sufficiently impressed by my apparel and demeanour.

"Ahem." The butler reappeared at the parlour door, and while he looked as disapproving as ever, he told me, "Lady Theodora is not dressed to receive you in the morning-room, but she wonders whether you would care to step into her boudoir for a few moments."

Ah. Just as I had hoped. Although I must now proceed with the greatest delicacy.

Following the butler upstairs, I heard youthful voices issuing from a nursery on the floor above, where a nanny, or perhaps a governess, attempted to civilise the Alistair children. The Honourable Lady Cecily, according to *Boyles*, had no less than seven brothers and sisters.

Such being the case, it is amazing how youthful in appearance Lady Theodora turned out to be. Or perhaps such was the effect of her grief plus her perfectly lovely, lacy tea-frock. A recent fad instigated by the artwork of Kate Greenaway, tea-frocks allowed one to go without a corset when receiving (female only!) visitors in one's personal rooms. In the high-waisted, comfortable, very pretty garment, Lady Theodora appeared charming and almost childlike, whereas I would have looked a proper stork in one.

She did not immediately turn to me as I stepped in at the door. With maids in fluttering attendance, fussing with her long curls of auburn hair, she remained upon a dainty chair facing her dressing-table, powdering her tear-stained face, so that I saw her first in the mirror.

Our eyes met in a glass darkly, as it were.

Remembering to be bashful, I glanced away.

I am sure she took a good long look at me while I stood gazing up and around like a tourist in a European cathedral. Actually, the room was rather similar to Mum's at home—light and airy with Japanese screens and furniture carved in the delicate Oriental fashion. Not so grand. But I must seem awed. *Timid*, I reminded myself mentally. *Married young, naïve and terribly plain. No threat to anyone.*

"That will do." Turning, Lady Theodora shrugged off a filmy combing-jacket and shooed the servants away with her hands. "Mrs. Ragostin, please sit down."

I perched on the edge of a settee. "My, um, apologies for intruding upon you in this, um, that is to say, unseemly manner, quite without a proper introduction, Lady Alistair, and at such a difficult . . ." I allowed my barely audible murmurings to trail away in a pretense of confusion because I, a stranger, was not supposed to know that this was a difficult time for her. Although she knew perfectly well that I did know; why else would I be there?

She spared me further pretense. "Your husband sent you, Mrs. Ragostin?"

I lifted my lowered eyes to Lady Theodora's pretty face—no, beautiful: This was a beautiful woman. Somewhat square of jaw and full of mouth, but with brilliant eyes, her expression remarkably cultured and sensitive. A society lady who was not usually so direct, I imagined. Much more the type to play the game of social dissembling to its fullest, dealing in hints and intimations and coyness. Only extremity could drive her to be so blunt.

"Um, yes," I faltered. "Dr. Ragostin felt that it would be indelicate for him to—to venture here himself, you know . . ."

Once more the stumbling halt, allowing her the choice, whether to speak of that which the whole world knew but was not supposed to know.

Lady Theodora stiffened for only a moment before she nodded. I have often noticed how a proud and beautiful woman will find a friend in one who is plain, quiet, and humble. "Yes," she said in a low voice, "my daughter, Lady Cecily, seems to have—that is—I, or rather, we, her parents, don't know where she is. Am I correct to understand that your husband finds persons who have gone missing?"

"Yes, quite so."

"He is offering his services?"

"If you wish. But with no expectation of reward, my lady."

"Indeed." She did not believe this; she thought it more than likely that Dr. Ragostin was opportunistic and a sham, but at the same time—

She said it. "I am desperate, Mrs. Ragostin." Watching my face, she spoke with deliberate control, but I could see her trembling. "There has been no news of my daughter—none!—for a week, and the authorities seem utterly ineffectual. Surely your husband can do no worse. No doubt I am being a fool, for I am under orders to summon no one on my own, but I can hardly be blamed if you have come to *me*. I cannot help feeling that a providential God may have sent you here, however self-serving—not you personally, I mean, but your husband—no offense intended."

"None taken, I assure you, Lady Theodora." I allowed my shy, apologetic gaze to drift towards her. "Most preposterous, my being here, but husbands *will* have their way."

I could not have struck a stronger empathic chord in her. "Oh, Mrs. Ragostin!" She actually leaned forward to clasp my gloved hands. "How true! The men run everything, yet they are so *wrong!* In my heart I know that my Cecily has not—would not go anywhere they say she has. And the fact that they have not found her shows me to be correct. Yet they persist in believing . . . How awful. Even my husband . . ."

I nodded, thinking ahead to guide the conversation without, I hoped, her noticing. "Is your husband very much older than you are, Lady Theodora?"

"Only a few years. But—is Dr. Ragostin greatly your senior?"

"Yes. I am his third wife. Why, I am not much older than . . ."

She said it for me. Whispered it, actually. "Than my daughter. Lady Cecily."

"Indeed. Quite. Therefore, I was thinking . . ."

"Yes?" Already we had become co-conspirators; our knees almost touched, she sat so close to me, clinging to my hands.

"I wonder if, as a girl of Lady Cecily's age, I might notice something that the police detectives have overlooked . . ."

"Oh, how I wish you would, Mrs. Ragostin! I have been longing to do something . . . but what? And how?"

I almost forgot to play my role, but remembered in time to hesitate, biting my lip, before I said, "Well . . . one must start somewhere. If it is at all possible, Lady Theodora, might I examine Lady Cecily's rooms?"

CHAPTER THE SIXTH

FIRST, OF COURSE, WE TOOK TEA. THEN, complicity and friendship sealed over the soothing hot beverage and its accompanying marmalade tarts, Lady Theodora called for Lady Cecily's personal maid, who escorted me to the Honourable Lady Cecily's rooms.

The usual thing for gentry is to have one's bed in a room with a dressing-closet, behind another room where servants and friends come in and out. I walked straight through to look at Lady Cecily's bedchamber, and it appeared at first glance to be sweetness itself, with a carved and daintily painted sleigh bed, more suitable, I thought, for a girl than for a young lady. Perhaps her mum had tried to keep her a baby? In a corner sat the usual dollhouse, meant to encourage domestic pride, but it did not look as if Lady Cecily enjoyed that sort of thing any better than I did. Her expensive china and porcelain dolls stood neglected on their shelves, dusty even inside their glass cases. Nor, I thought, glancing at similar glass "bells" on the mantelpiece, did she enjoy the genteel craft of moulding roses out of coloured wax.

"Did Lady Cecily make those herself?" I asked the maid to be sure.

"Yes, ma'am. My young lady was—ah, is—well versed in all handicrafts."

The wax "flowers" looked more like shapeless blobs.

On the walls hung small, framed pastels: old woman knitting by the fire, country maiden with a basket of eggs, rosy-cheeked child holding a puppy, et cetera.

"Did Lady Cecily draw those?"

"Yes, ma'am. Lady Cecily is quite the artist."

Debatable, I thought even as I nodded. The pastels, like the wax flowers, appeared colourful but uncertain, their lines and forms much blurred.

"Lady Cecily has had voice lessons, too, and ballet. In every way she is most accomplished."

Fit for the marriage market, in other words, as

my brothers wanted me to be: a singing, dancing, French-quoting, delicately fainting decoration to any aristocratic drawing-room.

I wondered how Lady Cecily felt about her "accomplishments."

Aside from the sleigh bed, I saw a similarly ornate wardrobe, a dresser, and a washstand in the young lady's bedroom. On the dresser stood the usual "set": ring-stand, silver-embossed comb and brush, hand mirror, cut-glass toilet water bottles, hair tidy. I glanced into the wardrobe, scanning the usual apparel of an aristocratic miss: morning-dresses, afternoon-dresses, visiting-dresses, Sunday best, evening-gowns, riding habit, cycling costume, tennis-dress, ad infinitum. "Has it been ascertained what Lady Cecily was wearing at the time of her, ah, departure?"

"Yes, ma'am. It would seem that she . . ." The maid blushed. "She was garbed for slumber, ma'am. Nothing else is missing."

"Indeed. Was her bed slept in?"

"Yes, ma'am."

One window faced the back of the house, and one faced the side. "At which of these was the ladder placed?"

The maid indicated the one at the back of the house, out of view of the street.

"And the window was found open?"

"Yes, ma'am."

"Were any windows or doors downstairs opened?"

"No, ma'am. The downstairs doors were locked and barred, and the windows snibbed."

"But these windows were not snibbed?"

"No, ma'am." The maid sounded as if she pitied my ignorance. "To improve their health, all members of the baronet's family sleep with the window slightly raised, ma'am, winter or summer, ma'am."

Unsurprising; I myself had been raised the same way. Ventilation strengthened the moral resolve of one's digestion and so forth against disease, and guarded one's personage against laxness. Therefore, even during the coldest weather, fit to frost one's nightcap, a window had to be left open an inch or so.

"So the window sash could have been raised by someone on the ladder outside."

"Yes, ma'am."

"And it was left that way, wide open, with the ladder at the sill?"

"Yes, ma'am."

I backtracked into Lady Cecily's boudoir, a sizable room lavished with mirrors, chairs, settees, a needlepoint fire-screen (Lady Cecily's accomplishment, no doubt), potted ferns in the bay window, and near that source of light, Lady Cecily's easel and art stand.

And—I thought, at the time, more important—a roll-top desk.

I opened the desk first. "Some letters were found in here, I understand?"

"Yes, ma'am. The police took them, ma'am."

"Did they search this desk for other documents?"

"No, ma'am!" The maid sounded shocked. "Lady Theodora discovered the letters and took them downstairs to the officers."

In other words, no detective had been allowed to set foot in these rooms.

"Quite so," I said approvingly as I seated myself at the desk to have a look.

Fervidly I wished I could have seen the letters themselves, not only for content but also for any indications Scotland Yard might have overlooked. "Were the postage-stamps positioned oddly, or reversed?" If so, it would suggest a code.

"The letters did not come through the *post*,

ma'am!" I had shocked the maid again. Probably the formidable butler oversaw all postal correspondence.

"How so, then?" By hand, obviously, but by whose hand?

"We, ah, we do not know. Ma'am."

With the complicity of one of the servants, in other words. Perhaps this very maid, Lily by name. And that line of inquiry had already been exhausted.

The surface of the desk was occupied by an exquisite writing set, ink-bottle and fountain pens, pen-holder and letter-opener all of jade. In the drawers, along with the usual blotting-paper, pen-wipers and such, I found the lady's monogrammed stationery and several sticks of sealing-wax in different colours: red for business correspondence, blue for constancy in love, grey for friendship, yellow for jealousy, green for encouragement of a shy lover, violet for condolences. But only the grey stick of wax looked much used.

Also in the drawers I found Lady Cecily's address-book, well kept in the petite, curlicue handwriting of an aristocratic miss. I found sundry other papers: shopping lists, reminders of social obligations, moral exhortations themed around the letters of the alphabet, that sort of thing.

Much more important, I found a stack of journals.

"Lady Cecily kept diaries?" The silk-covered volumes were equipped with tiny padlocks.

"Yes, ma'am."

But the padlocks had been broken open. "Did the police look at these?"

"No, ma'am!"

"Lady Theodora, then?"

"Yes, ma'am. In the mirror, ma'am."

"I beg your pardon?" But as I spoke, I took one of the books, opened it, and gawked at the handwriting therein. Large, childishly plain, and all slanted leftward—utterly unlike the handwriting of the address book and other papers—it made no sense to me until I realised it was *written* from right to left, its words running from right to left with even their letters reversed, so that *b* looked like *∂*.

"How very peculiar!" I exclaimed. Getting up, I held the diary open towards a standing mirror, in which I could easily read,

*most frightfully cold. I am wearing no less
than nine petticoats*

As a cipher, this backwards writing was hardly
worth bothering with.

"Why in the world did she write that way?"

"I don't know, ma'am."

"Did you ever see her do it?"

"No, ma'am."

Like any loyal servant, of course she had
seen nothing.

There were eight diaries, all of them in the same
odd leftward writing, unchanged over a period of
years. Settling upon the most recent diary, the only
one with blank pages at the—the beginning, actually, as the diaries had been written from the back
towards the front—I turned to the last (first) entry,
then held it to the mirror and read.

*January 2—I am so dreadfully bored.
How can anyone talk of New Year's
Resolutions when no amount of good intentions seems ever to alleviate the suffering in this world? And how can they*

chatter of perfumes and parties, flounces and necklines and dancing slippers when the streets swarm with orphans and pauper children who have barely even rags to wear, nor shoes for their feet? While their fathers cannot find work and their mothers labour sixteen hours a day in the mills? And while I, in order to be presented to the Queen, practice walking backwards without tripping over a nine-foot train? Mine is a life without any worthwhile purpose, without value, empty of meaning.

Hardly the sentiments of a young woman about to elope with her secret lover!

With a mind full of conjecture I left Lily to replace items in the desk while I crossed the room to see what Lady Cecily had been drawing lately.

On her easel I found an undersized and unfinished pastel of a country landscape, already turning into a shapeless mass of candy-coloured smudge. Atop her art stand lay her pastels.

Broken. Pink, peach, pale green, aqua, sky blue, lavender, powdery brown, all broken to jagged bits.

Most interesting.

I pulled open the drawer of her art stand, finding about what one might expect: pencils, eraser, India ink and art pens still in their box, and—not in a box—sticks of charcoal. Stubs, rather, with blunted tips, dirtying all the contents of the drawer with black powder the way soot besmirched London city. Quantities of charcoal lay everywhere.

Worn to nubbins.

I blinked at the pastel daub on the easel, not a hint of black in it anywhere.

I looked around at the walls and found them innocent of any dark artwork.

After closing the drawer, I crossed to where the maid was tidying the desk. "Lily, where are Lady Cecily's charcoal drawings?"

"Charcoal?" Moving the jade items of the lady's writing set from one end of the desk to the other, she would not look at me. "I am sure I have no idea, ma'am."

I was equally sure that she did, but there was no

use saying so. Instead, imagining where I would put artwork if I didn't want anyone to see it, I went back into the lady's bedchamber and started peering behind furniture.

In back of both the dresser and the wardrobe I could see sheets of heavy paper, quite large, leaning against the wall.

"Lily," I called, "you'd better help me get these out, unless you want me to smear them."

Silently, sullenly, the girl came and helped me push the furniture a few inches away from the walls, so that I could reach behind. Taking the papers by their edges, I carried them to the other room in order to look at them in the light.

One by one I placed them upon the easel, where their size dwarfed that of the pastel.

Not only their size. Their — I scarcely know how to explain. Their temper, one might call it. Nothing could have been more unlike the pinky-bluey blurs that had been framed to hang on the walls. These charcoal drawings were rendered in heavy black strokes, knife-sharp and direct, shockingly unsoftened by any shading.

But the subjects were even more shocking.

Scrawny, filthy children playing in a gutter
beneath a clothesline strung with dead fish.
Hatless women standing under a street-lamp
at night to sew.
An unshaven man picking up cigar butts.
An Italian family singing for pennies.
A barefoot boy kneeling on the cobbles to shine
a gentleman's boots.
A ragged woman with a sickly baby "selling"
matches door-to-door.

And many more.

People from the poorest streets of London.

People depicted so boldly, so surely, with such unblinking honesty that they could not possibly have been done from imagination. One who was born to be an artist had seen them to draw them. I knew that feeling of fiery connection between eyes and heart and hand. An inspired artist had looked upon these people.

With passion.

As I looked upon them with passion.

Several of the drawings showed starving old women dozing on the workhouse steps. The poorest of the poor, these "crawlers" or "dosses" seldom found strength to move.

I knew them.

And so, evidently, did Lady Cecily.

But how?

CHAPTER THE SEVENTH

"Dr. Ragostin will contact you discreetly," I told Lady Theodora, "with his thoughts upon the matter."

It was fortunate that "Dr. Ragostin" was to supply the thoughts, for mine were in a muddle worse than the most tangled yarn basket that ever was. Out of all the Gordian knot I seized upon only one strand surely, a grey one, another indication that Lady Cecily had *not* eloped. If her secret correspondence with the shopkeeper's son had developed into a passionate affair, she would have used a rainbow of sealing-wax other than the grey. No, she had written her letters only in friendship.

She had gone off not for love, but for some other reason.

Which, I sensed, had something to do with her odd diaries. The mirror writing.

And something—although I could not even begin to imagine what—something to do with her extraordinary charcoal drawings.

The latter were so unladylike and disturbing, both in their bold execution and in their choice of subjects, that I had put them back behind the bedroom furniture and had not mentioned them to Lady Theodora. Not yet, if ever. The diaries, however, I wished to take with me.

"For my eyes only," I assured the lady when I had a chance to speak with her privately. Reporting to her dressing-room, I had found her busy with the younger children, two little boys and a little girl romping around her chamber like puppies while she inspected a somewhat older girl for kempt hair, cleanly ears, et cetera. The girl's face reminded me very much of Lady Cecily as I had seen her in the photographic portraits Lady Theodora had showed me over tea. Indeed, all of the children, including Lady Cecily, much resembled their mother—generous mouth, brilliant, intelligent eyes.

Lady Theodora shooed the young Alistairs back

to the care of their governess when I came in, and beckoned for me to sit close to her.

"I will myself read the diaries," I explained to her after making my request, "and inform Dr. Ragostin in the most discreet terms of any indications I may find."

"I have looked through them," Lady Theodora responded, "and found nothing that seemed harmful, but by all means, if you think it will help—you will take the greatest care of them?"

I assured her I would, remembering just in time to ask her also for a recent portrait of Lady Cecily so that "Dr. Ragostin" could see what the missing miss looked like. Also, I copied down the name and address of the shopkeeper's son with whom Lady Cecily had been corresponding, in case "Dr. Ragostin" wished to question him.

As I departed, Lady Theodora embraced me, kissing my cheek with the most unexpected strength of feeling.

Therefore I felt quite wretched, like a shameful fraud, as I took a cab back to Dr. Ragostin's office. Dr. Ragostin this, Dr. Ragostin that; I was a liar, and finding this lost girl was up to—me? A runaway upstart of fourteen? True, half the domestics and mill-hands in London were my age or younger, and true, also, that any of us who committed a crime would be imprisoned, tried, and hanged right along with Jack the Ripper should the police ever find him — but we had no rights, none, not even a right to the money we earned, until we turned twenty-one. Legally, at age fourteen I did not yet exist. So who on Earth did I think I was — Enola Ivy Holmes Meshle Mrs. Ragostin — to attempt the monstrous hoax that was my life?

Such were my thoughts as I slipped through the secret entry into the locked room where I transformed myself back into Ivy Meshle. My subdued frame of mind lasted through the rest of the afternoon into the evening, when I returned to my lodging with Lady Cecily's casement photograph and journals done up, as if I had been shopping, in a brown paper parcel tied with string.

After Mrs. Tupper had provided me with a meal of herring stewed with parsnips — most unhelpful to one attempting to grow plump — I retreated upstairs to my room, made myself comfortable in warm socks and a dressing-gown, settled myself in my armchair by the hearth, and with the aid of a hand mirror began to read Lady Cecily's most recent diary.

The content was not at all what one might expect from a baronet's daughter. I found nothing about Sunday phaeton rides in Hyde Park, holidays at the seaside, shopping along Regent Street, the latest fashions in millinery, or even a mention of a new dress. Nor did I find any accounts of her diversions with her friends. Instead, the entries were mostly troubled musings:

. . . *a great deal of talk about the Poor Law, the "deserving poor" versus those who are undeserving. Unfortunates who have been blinded, crippled, et cetera through no fault of their own are regarded as worthy of charitable aid, but all of those who are physically able, Daddy says, must be morally deficient, lazy, and undeserving of consideration; the beggars should continue to be whipped out of town as has been the custom, or else go to the workhouse. But if work is such a great good, why, then, does the workhouse pun-*

ish its inmates with dinners of thin gruel after their long hours of the hardest possible labour?

. . . social Darwinism and the survival of the fittest would hold that there is no such category as "deserving" poor. Those who have showed themselves unable to support themselves should be let alone as Nature takes its course, eliminating them, making way for a superior human race. Of which we of the titled classes, I suppose, are examples? Because we can quote Shakespeare, play Chopin upon the piano, and keep our gloves clean while taking tea?

What of the babies? For the most part, the poverty-stricken people who are succumbing to Darwin's selective process have already reproduced. By this way of thinking, should the babies also be abandoned to perish?

. . . the Great Unwashed of the East End are not themselves intellectually capable of organising unions and marches, Daddy declares; some outside influence, very likely foreign and enemy, must be to blame for the disturbances, and the police are fully justified in bloodying heads in order to put a halt to any further and more serious uprisings. He does not deny that the mill-workers live in fever-nests unfit for pigs and toil until they fall down, like galley-slaves under the whips of heartless foremen—but he does not seem to feel that they deserve any better. He does not seem to feel that they are people like us at all. It is so difficult for me to sit and fold my hands in my lap, smile sweetly and listen . . .

After reading this and much more, I still considered myself a fraud, for my weary brain, while sympathetic to Lady Cecily's point of view, could make nothing practical of it.

Slumber, I decided, was needful. Sleep would knit up the ravelled sleave of care, to quote some Shakespeare myself. Or, in this case, sleep would tidy my yarn-basket mind.

Thus, without admitting that I was afraid, I excused myself from venturing forth in habit and black cowl that night. Instead, I went to bed.

Awakening what seemed like a moment afterward, I found that it was morning.

Somehow, while I had slept so soundly—unusual for me—the muddle in my mind had indeed sorted itself out a bit, so that a thread of reasoning presented itself to me, thus:

I had come to London; I had seen London's poor; I had felt impelled to help them.

Lady Cecily, by the evidence of her charcoal drawings, also had seen. I did not yet know how this highly irregular encounter had come to pass, nor did I know whether it had happened before or after her questioning journal entries, but somehow (and I must find out how) the young lady had walked amongst London's poor.

Had she also felt impelled to help them?

Had she perhaps left home of her own free will?

. . .

Settling into my office to "work" as Ivy Meshle, I read the morning newspapers. Finding no communication from Mum, I tossed the news of the day into the fire, then rang for tea.

Meanwhile, in a contemplative frame of mind, I got out Lady Cecily's photographic portrait and a sheaf of foolscap paper. Referring to the portrait, I pencilled a quick likeness of the lady. Then, putting the photograph away, I drew her head in profile, recalling other photographs I had seen of her, combining those memories with my observations of her mother and brothers and sisters, all of whom so strongly resembled one another. Over and over again I sketched Lady Cecily, with no aristocratic finery, just her face, from various angles until I began to feel that I had met her in person.

Deep in my work, I had not noticed Joddy entering the office with my tea. Unaware of the boy's presence, I jumped when his piping voice spoke from behind my shoulder: "I didn't know you could draw like that!"

It was not his place to comment, but luckily it took me a startled moment to catch my breath before I told him so. And in that moment he spoke again. "I know 'er," he declared, setting down the tea-tray, then pointing at my portraits of Lady Cecily with his stubby white-gloved forefinger.

Ridiculous. He could not possibly—

Wait a minute.

"Indeed?" I tried not to show how interested I was, for like any servant he would draw himself into a shell if I questioned him too sharply. I kept my tone carefully neutral. "What is her name?"

"I don't know 'er like *that*. I've seen her some-place, is all."

"Where, pray tell?"

"I don't remember."

I swivelled to observe him. There he stood with a faraway gaze, as if trying to recall a dream.

"Was she in a carriage?"

He shook his head slowly, looking puzzled, be-fore he remembered his manners. "No, my—no, Miss Meshle. She were standing on a corner, like."

"Where? Piccadilly, Trafalgar Square, Seven Dials?"

"I don't know."

"Well then, doing what? Shopping?"

"No, I don't think so . . ." Uncertain.

My patience beginning to wear thin, I grumbled,

"Selling matches?" A ridiculous notion, for only beggars sold matches.

But, looking mildly startled, Joddy murmured, "Matches. Strike."

Bean-headed boy, of course one struck a match in order to light it. Restraining myself from rolling my eyes, and trying to keep my impatience out of my tone, I tried another question. "What was she wearing?"

Of course he did not answer what I had asked. "She 'ad somethin' in a basket," he said.

As did half the populace of London, I thought, and the other half had something in a barrow. Common folk lived penny-in-hand to pastry-in-mouth, most of them, lacking icebox to keep food or stove to prepare dinner, eating sooty messes they bought from street vendors, the poor living off the poor. "Something in a basket? What?" I asked, utterly surprised and a bit sarcastic, for surely the flea-brained boy had to be mistaken. "Roly-poly puddings?"

"No, Miss Meshle, nothin' like that. I think it were papers."

"You think you saw this girl selling *newspapers*?"

I should have kept my mouth closed, or at the very least, my tone under better control.

"No, my—um, no, Miss Meshle." Frightened into stupidity, Joddy would be of no further use.

Indeed, after a few more attempts, I found that there was nothing more to be got out of him. "That will do. Thank you, Joddy."

After he had left, I muttered several naughty things in a low tone, then dismissed the episode from my mind. The frustrating, addlepated boy had probably seen some other pretty girl.

Sipping my tea and, I admit, admiring my own artwork for a few minutes before I burned it in the fire, I continued to mull over the matter of the missing Lady Cecily.

I discarded the absurd notion that she had eloped, for reasons already mentioned, and also because she would hardly have gone off in her nightgown! Rather, in preparation for such a romantic escapade, she would have been waiting in her most fetching frock.

But supposing her escapade, rather than being romantic, had involved any of the poorer neighborhoods of London—well, the essence remained the same: She would not have gone in a nightgown. Had she perhaps secreted some more humble apparel for herself, and hidden the nightgown to make it appear—

What? That she had been snatched from her bed by a kidnapper?

And forcibly carried down a ladder? Nonsense. Impossible, in my experience of ladders.

Had the ladder been placed at her window as a blind?

If she had gone away on her own, how had she travelled? Had anyone assisted her?

I had too many questions and not enough answers.

Presently I rang the bell again.

"Joddy," I told the boy-in-buttons when he appeared, "go fetch me a cab."

Miss Meshle was going shopping.

But not in any of the establishments I normally frequented. I had the cab, which cost sixpence a mile, drop me at the nearest railway station—much less expensive, as I had to travel some small distance, to a northern part of London where I particularly wanted to visit a certain commercial establishment: Ebenezer Finch & Son Emporium.

Exiting the train at St. Pancras Station—a frothy architectural confection if I ever saw one—I walked a few blocks. As Ivy Meshle, an ordinary office worker whose skirt, while decently concealing her ankles, did not trail in the dirt, I attracted leers instead of glares. This time the top-hatted gentlemen took no notice of me at all, and no one suggested it would be my own fault if I came to harm—but male clerks ogled from shop doorways, and a working-class loiterer spoke to me: "'Ow do you do, sweet-'eart? What's yer 'urry? Stop an' chat a bit."

Pretending I had not heard, without so much as a glance I strode past him. Thank goodness he did not follow, as had been known to happen. Indeed, a slop-girl walking in the slums enjoyed more peace than any decent female on city streets. I found it necessary to ignore several other male pests before I finally spied my destination.

Approaching Ebenezer Finch & Son Emporium, I felt my eyes widen, for never had I seen such capacious bow windows flanking the door of a shop, or so many polished brass dress forms upon which were displayed the latest strait-belted fashions. In, I might add, the most startling of chemically derived colours.

Walking inside provided even more of a shock to my sensibilities. One must understand that shopping as I knew it consisted of entering a stationer's dark little establishment, or an apothecary's, or a draper's, for instance, and telling the fusty black-suited man behind the counter what of his particular merchandise one wanted, upon which he would either bring an item forth from storage or else take down an order. Shopping was logical and dull. But this Ebenezer Finch & Son Emporium, brilliantly gas-lit even in the daytime, was so far from dull that it arrested the logical workings of the mind. Its merchandise flaunted, attracted, distracted, dazed. On the panelled walls and the varnished wooden counter-tops and even hanging from the ceiling were displayed an astounding variety of wares: bolts of fabric and trimming; hats, gloves, and shawls; tools and padlocks; wooden toys and tin soldiers; kitchen cutlery of all sorts; buckets and watering-cans; caps and aprons and wrought-iron coat hooks, china figurines, fancy-ware, flowers and ribbons, swags of lace and chiffon—it was as if I had stepped into an ocular whirlpool.

At first, saturated with colour, sheen, and flutter, I could scarcely make sense of my surroundings. It was as if everywhere I looked, something shiny attempted to steal away my vital principle like a Mesmerist's watch winking on its chain. But exerting an effort of will to sort out the spectacle before me, I began to notice that different categories of items were stored and displayed in different areas attended by different clerks—many of them female clerks, I saw with relief—behind counters that seemed to stretch for a mile. The shop was necessarily quite large, scarcely to be called a shop at all; indeed, this was my first experience of what came to be known as a "department" store.

I wondered what constant exposure to this place might do to those who worked here. Hatters went mad and painters became poisoned; labourers in cotton mills grew stunted if they did not sicken and die; this "emporium" also seemed somehow unhealthful to me. How might such a plethora of pretty things affect, if not the body, then the mind?

In a prominent position just inside the door was displayed a photographic portrait of the proprietor, Ebenezer Finch, & Son. Once I had managed to rein in my runaway thoughts, I studied this likeness with interest, not so much in Ebenezer Finch as in Son.

Alexander Finch.

Shopkeeper's son of impudent fame, alleged seducer of Lady Cecily Alistair.

CHAPTER THE EIGHTH

WITHIN THE ORNATELY FRAMED PHOTO-graph he appeared ordinary enough—indeed, so nondescript as to give one the impression that one had seen him somewhere before. An effect no doubt produced by the blankness of expression that is required in order to hold a pose for a camera.

Wandering further into the kaleidoscopic depths of the shop, I looked about me, ostensibly for something to buy, but actually for Mr. Alexander Finch.

I wanted to assess him. To arrive at some conclusion concerning his character. To guess at the degree of his involvement, if any, in Lady Cecily's disappearance.

As luck would have it, I found him almost immediately, for a loud, hectoring voice caught my attention. "Alexander, a monkey could dress them windows better!"

Looking towards the source of this ungrammatical statement, I located an office — rather an octopus affair, with pneumatic payment-and-receipt tubes running into it from all areas of the store — evidently the proprietor's office, elevated in the emporium's farthest corner. Through its large windows, presumably meant for keeping an eye on commerce, I could see Ebenezer Finch haranguing his son.

". . . sort of colours one would expect from a screaming anarchist," the father was blustering as he stabbed an accusing finger at his son. "Get them changed to something more tasteful straightaway."

"Yes, sir." Standing with his hands folded in front of him, the younger Finch showed not the least emotion, not even a trace of angry red in his face.

"But you're not to set foot an inch beyond the doorstep, do you hear me?"

"Yes, sir."

"Expedite the matter, and tell me when you're done."

Dismissed, Mr. Alexander Finch gave a nod and exited the office.

By taking a few quick strides, I contrived to encounter him at the bottom of the brass-railed stairs leading down to the main floor of the store. Rather breathlessly I addressed him, "Excuse me, Mr. Finch . . ."

"May I help you, miss?" Halting to face me, he seemed pleasant and obliging enough. A bit dandified, perhaps. He wore tinted eyeglasses indoors. And instead of the usual sober garb of a clerk, he had on a peacock-blue ascot with a horseshoe pin, a silver-grey waistcoat with white buttons, and very smart cuff-links; indeed, his was the male equivalent of the fashionable but inexpensive clothing that ornamented Miss Meshle. If he were a seducer, perhaps he would show some interest in me—

Nonsense. Any comparison to me was hardly fair to Lady Cecily, who was not giraffe-like in personage.

I told Alexander Finch, "Sir, I find myself quite bewildered by such a palatial establishment graced by such a variety of wares, and I wonder whether you might show me . . ." Then I let my voice sink to a murmur only he could hear. "Lady Theodora Alistair sent me to speak with you."

My heart quickened as I watched to see how he would react.

But he barely reacted at all, showing only the faintest flicker of surprise, from which he recovered quickly, falling in with my charade. "If you'll just walk this way, miss, I'll be pleased to assist you."

He led me back through the store, past a counter where an attractive female clerk stood behind absurdly disembodied carved wooden hands displaying gloves, past another where a spinsterish woman exhibited cast-iron hearth sets to husband and wife; past several more, until he reached one where a willowy young working girl stood. To her he said, "Disappear."

Although his tone was low and neutral, she fled wide-eyed without a smile or a word—in fear? But perhaps such was her usual manner with him. She was, after all, a doe-eyed young thing, and he was the master's son.

Himself slipping behind the now-vacant counter, Mr. Alexander Finch told me, "Here we have the very latest fashions in ladies' footwear."

It would have attracted attention, you see, appearing disreputable, had I simply stood and talked with him. But we could converse over a countertop, and to any onlooker it would seem that he was strictly attending to business, waiting upon me.

I wasted no time. "Lady Theodora is taking matters into her own hands," I explained, or fictionalised, "to see what the fair sex, in an unofficial way, can accomplish in searching for the missing Lady Cecily."

"Quite so. Something for spring, you say?" Pulling open some of the many deep drawers beneath and behind the counter, he brought forth a fawn-coloured boot with a delicate heel, a pearl-grey one that buttoned up the front instead of the side, and a tan one with laces.

The boots were of excellent quality and quite lovely, but I only pretended to look at them as I told him, "No doubt you think it foolish, but Lady Theodora feels we must try. You see, the police have been of no help."

"I'd say not. All they do is watch me, and my father's so vexed with me, he won't let me out the door."

He said this just as imperturbably as he'd said anything else. So far I had gained no sense of him, none at all, whether for good or for ill.

"Do you live at home with your parents?" I asked for lack of any better question.

"No, I stay with the other clerks."

No doubt in a dormitory above the store.

"Well, you've some respite from your father's vexation, then. Why is he angry with you?"

"Because I forget my place, as he calls it, treating people all much the same." He gestured towards a bentwood chair placed on my side of the counter. "Would you care to have a seat, my lady?"

"Oh, no!" I sat rather abruptly, because my knees weakened. "I am not—I don't—such a title—"

"Well, the quality of your speech says you're not what you appear to be, either."

While not titled by birth, certainly not one to be presented at court, I was a squire's daughter, and as such, a member of the gentry, one who does not work for money. And my accent, if not my clothing, betrayed my rank. Sitting with my mouth airing, I scolded myself internally: *I must be more careful.* This was why I had decided the nocturnal Sister must be a mute—because my distinctive voice might give me away.

At the same time I began to understand why Lady Cecily might have entered into correspondence with this young man. Beneath his bland exterior lay a great deal of intelligence and—and some other, less definable qualities.

Indeed, for a moment I felt quite uncomfortable as he leaned on his elbows studying me through his tinted spectacles, which made it difficult for me to see his eyes or read their expression.

Just as I started to turn away from his scrutiny, the young man almost smiled. For a moment there was a flicker of some realisation—knowledge, or triumph—in his smirk. He said, "I do believe we have met. What, may I ask, is your name?"

"Certainly you may ask," I told him, controlling my tone as best I could.

A moment passed before he understood that I would not answer. Then he seemed to drop the subject entirely. "I personally feel that boot-laces are far superior to buttons," he remarked, holding up the tan boot. "They obviate the tedium of a button-hook, and mould the leather more closely to the limb of the wearer." Which should not have been desirable or necessary, were the lower extremities not meant to be seen, after all, a glimpse now and then, as this young man knew quite well—though I felt a bit odd hearing him insinuate so. As he spoke, he yanked upon the laces to demonstrate their function, for all the world like a maid pulling upon stay-laces, giving the boot a wasp waist where an ankle should have been.

I barely looked. "Indeed." My attention remained on his round, blank, bespectacled face. "And if I am a lady, then would you consider yourself a gentleman?"

"Just my point. This country is mad for valuing people according to their titles." He continued to strait-lace the tan boot. "Why should an idle so-called aristocrat be considered more of a gentleman than any thrifty, sober, industrious member of the working class?"

As he spoke this outrageous nonsense, I sensed passion beneath his cool exterior.

Uncertain where it might lead, I asked cautiously, "You are in favour of democracy, then?" Shocking, if so, even to one who had been raised by a Suffragist.

But he replied, "I scorn all such labels." Indeed he almost sneered, setting down the tan boot, now appearing strangled in its own laces. "I pigeon-hole no one, I'll befriend anyone," (he said rather viciously,) "and if someone needs help, I'll help them, whether they're a scullery-maid or —"

The way he broke off gave me my cue. "Lady Cecily needed help?"

His hard voice lowered, if not exactly softening. "Flat tyre on her bicycle, that was all, when I was out running errands on mine, and I patched hers with my kit, and we got to talking."

"Alexander!" roared a male voice close at hand.

The young man in question lifted the delicate fawn-coloured boot. "To place an order, miss, all you need do is post us a tracing of your right foot—"

Mr. Ebenezer Finch hove into view, ranting, "Alexander, I told you—oh." He broke off rather ungraciously. "I see. You're helping a customer."

How very odd, I thought, that while the father was so choleric, the son appeared so stoical. More than stoical. Nearly wooden.

After his father departed, without acknowledging the interruption in the least the young man told me, "Lady Cecily was a serious sort of girl. She'd been reading *Das Kapital,* and we discussed the exploitation of the masses."

Das Kapital? I had heard whispers of the book — it was considered shocking, no, beyond shocking, Not Nice At All, simply deplorable. However, as with many such topics mentioned only in undertones—"life of ill repute," for instance—I had not the faintest idea what it was, actually.

However, Mr. Alexander Finch did not seem to require my comprehension in order to keep talking. "Lady Cecily considered our meeting most fortuitous. She wanted me to show her the proletariat."

Proletariat? A government building, perhaps?

"Not just domestics, clerks, and artisans, but the true toiling downtrodden factory-fodder masses," Mr. Alexander went on. "Naturally, I obliged her. We corresponded, and over a period of time—"

"Oh!" I interrupted.

"I beg your pardon, is something wrong?"

"Not at all." I had exclaimed because now I saw how Lady Cecily's charcoal drawings had come to be created. "You took her to the dock district, and the workhouse, and St. Giles, and the fish market at Billingsgate."

"How did you know that?" I saw a hint of a frown on his brow that had until now remained as smooth as new cheese. "Yes, exactly so. She would go bicycling with her friends, arranging to meet me, and I would escort her to see how most people in this world-famous city live."

Marx. I remembered now. An appalling man

named Karl Marx had written *Das Kapital*. "Lady Cecily was a *Marxist*?" I whispered, for this could not be spoken out loud.

"I have told you, I have no use for such labels." The young man's scorn of my intellectual capacity showed quite plainly.

"My apologies," I said meekly, for my upbringing as the disgrace of the Holmes family had made me quite accustomed to being looked down upon. (Literally so, in this case, as I sat in the bentwood chair and Alexander Finch stood behind the counter.) "I am sorry to trouble you with so many questions. Just let me ask you this: Why did Lady Cecily wish to see the, ah, proletariat?"

"Why, for education she could not obtain elsewhere, of course. She asked endless questions. Why were there so many pawn-shops. Why did the milkmaid lead a donkey behind her. What were 'drippings' and where did they come from. Why were children making bandboxes, and poor women sewing burlap sacks."

"But she must have wanted this knowledge for some reason. What were her plans?"

His tone, although still quite calm, became rather

less pleasant. "To make a whipping boy of me, by the look of things."

Not at all the answer I had expected. "Whatever do you mean?"

"Whatever could be plainer?" He mimicked my dismay. "She has gone off somewhere, while I take the blame."

Rather helplessly I suggested, "Perhaps she didn't realise you would be blamed."

"Why the ladder, then?"

I sat silent, knowing all too well why the ladder: so that Lady Cecily's family, aware of her only as a girl who drew sugary pastels, would think she had gone off with a seductive beau, silly young thing.

Whereas in truth, a young lady who read Marx might be capable of anything.

I asked Mr. Alexander Finch, "But did she not confide in you at all? Have you any idea where she has gone?"

"I don't know a thing about any of it," the young man said, arranging the boots so that they formed a straight line marching across the counter-top, "but what I think is, she walked right out the front door and put that ladder there herself."

Chapter the Ninth

ON MY WAY BACK TO ST. PANCRAS STATION I stopped at a bookshop. "*Das Kapital,* by Karl Marx," I told the portly gentleman behind the counter.

He did not move; indeed, he appeared to have, like various fairy-tale unfortunates, turned to stone, except for his mouth, which opened and closed several times.

"I assure you," I told him, "that after I have had a brief look inside it, I fully intend to cover it in baize and use it as a doorstop."

His mouth settled into a disapproving line before he spoke. "In English translation, miss, or in the original German?"

"In English, of course." Did I look like a scholar? Did I *sound* like one? Oh, dear, I *must* be more careful to control my gentrified accent, with which Alexander Finch had twitted me.

I did not at all know what to think of Alexander Finch. I had been able to read very little in his face, but his manner was odd at times. Never quite improper, but subtly peculiar. Yet I felt sympathy for him, subject as he was to his father's temper; I admired his stoicism, and I appreciated his willingness to speak frankly with me. His theory that Lady Cecily had left by the front door and placed a misleading ladder at her own window appealed to me; it was the sort of thing I would have done.

All in all, however, leaving the bookshop with my heavy parcel, I felt that I had not learned much.

And after scanning portions of *Das Kapital* that evening in the privacy of my lodging, I felt that—except for having learned what "proletariat" was, namely, the common people—other than that, I knew rather less than before. Lady Cecily, a convert to Marxism after reading this book? I had studied Hobbes, Darwin, even Winwood Reade's *Martyrdom of Man* with interest, but Marx—I must admit that Marx put me to sleep.

Quite soundly. I awoke the next morning wondering what sort of intellect Lady Cecily might possess, to be able to appreciate such rarefied rubbish.

And what, considering some of his rather shocking statements, Alexander Finch had been reading.

And if Lady Cecily had indeed marched out the door on her own, what had she worn, and where had she gone, and for what purpose?

But all such questions flew from my mind unresolved as I sat in my office sipping my morning tea and looking through the newspapers, for in the personal column of the *Pall Mall Gazette* I spied the following:

**245255   33151545   3315   4445154144
12432445244423   335144155133   21245215
45353424222345 333545231544**

Snatching for paper and pencil, I scrawled the alphabet in lines of five letters, then set to work.

245255. Second line, fourth letter, *I.* Fifth line, second letter, *V.* Fifth line, fifth letter, *Y.*

IVY.

It *was* for me!

Feverishly I worked on. Fully deciphered, the

message said, IVY MEET ME STEPS BRITISH MUSEUM FIVE TONIGHT MOTHER.

Oh.

Oh!

So quick, so sudden, just like that, to see my mother again? I felt as if my heart had stopped.

And just as quickly it started again, beating hard and quick like a regimental drum, as a thick porridge of conflicting emotions stirred through me. I loved Mum. I hated her. She had abandoned me. She had rescued me. She didn't love me. But she had given me freedom, by slipping me a great deal of money and also by the way she had raised me. Her stubborn independence, her adamant championing of women's rights—

Wait a minute.

IVY MEET ME STEPS BRITISH MUSEUM FIVE TONIGHT MOTHER.

The British Museum? That despised institution? Mum loathed the British Museum for its continual insults to female scholars. "Steps British Museum" seemed a most unlikely place for her to choose for a rendezvous.

And in that moment, the moment doubt entered

my mind, I discovered that, contrary emotions notwithstanding, I *wanted* to see my mother. Yearned to. I quite desperately tried to believe the message anyway, telling myself that Mum had simply chosen the British Museum because it was a convenient meeting place, centrally located in a respectable area of the city.

But at the same time I could almost hear her remembered voice inside my head adjuring me, *Enola, think*.

I thought.

And my thoughts provided no comfort. This message did not use our code of flowers in any way. Mum would not have said "meet me"—she would have made some reference to either the scarlet pimpernel or the mistletoe, both longtime symbols of a tryst. She would not have said "Mother." Instead, she would have said "your chrysanthemum," meaning Mum.

Inescapable conclusion: This message had not been placed in the newspaper by her.

But I still wanted to believe it *must* have been Mum. Who else could have—

Oh, no.

I knew who.

And thinking of him, my too-clever brother, I needed to say something quite naughty. "Oh, my stars and *garters*!"

Such was my degree of perturbation that it was difficult to keep presence of mind. I managed to muster that valuable commodity just sufficiently to scan the rest of the personal advertisements in all of the newspapers. In case there might really be something from Mum.

There was not, of course. Indeed, it was a bit too soon; previous missives had taken a week or more to arrive. While I had no idea how or where the Gypsies wintered, I pictured Mum somewhere far out in the countryside, requiring time to receive her publications by mail, decipher my message, check the train schedules, and post a reply.

And as she would be coming into London by rail, would she not have asked me to meet her at, or near, some railway station? Surely she would.

British Museum, humbug. Whoever had placed that advertisement had his own considerations in mind, not Mum's.

Whoever? Humph. I knew well enough that it was Sherlock.

Although it took me a few hours, and a headache,

to hypothesise how this disturbing turn of events might have come about, then decide what to do.

Luckily Dr. Ragostin's excellent secretary had kept Dr. John Watson's address.

Early in the afternoon, I took a cab to that worthy physician's office, finding myself let out in front of a modest practice-and-residence on a side street of northwest London.

A page whom Joddy could have emulated for manners showed me into a small, slightly shabby waiting-room and told me that the doctor was currently out but should return soon, for his consulting-hours began at one. The casement clock in the corner read a quarter till that hour. I was glad to wait.

As the clock chimed one, a stout old woman with a goiter and a uniformed commissionaire with a limp joined me in the waiting-room. However, I was let into the doctor's consulting-room first.

Like his waiting-room, it was small and just a trifle thread-worn about the upholstery and draperies.

"Miss, um . . ." Standing up behind his desk to greet me, the kind-eyed doctor recognised me, but could not place me.

"Miss Meshle, from Dr. Ragostin's office."

"Miss Meshle!" His smile lighted his otherwise commonplace face, making it positively charming. "Do sit down." He motioned me into the patient's chair and seated himself behind his desk again. "And what may I thank for this unexpected pleasure?"

So open and friendly was his manner that I believe I actually blushed. I would have adored this man for a father.

Until that moment, although I had often thought how nice it would be to have a friend or — or family, I suppose, not eccentric and scattered but real family that spent evenings reading in the parlour — still, I hadn't realised I would have liked to have a father. My own father had passed away when I was four years old, and until that moment I hadn't particularly missed him.

But I did now.

"I, um, am afraid, that is, I must not take up much of your time," I told Dr. Watson, faltering a bit from surprise at my own feelings. "Dr. Ragostin has, ah, reviewed your case and, um, sent me to ask you a question."

"By all means. I am delighted to hear of his interest. Just yesterday I was saying to myself that I must stop by his office and inquire . . . but now here you are. Please do go on."

"Dr. Ragostin would like to know, has Mr. Sherlock Holmes been following certain ciphers in the personal columns of the *Pall Mall Gazette*?"

"Holmes always reads the 'agony columns' in all of the major newspapers," Watson replied.

"Yes, but any ciphers in particular? Did you notice anything upon his desk, for instance, when you visited him?"

"Oh, yes, but that had nothing to do with the newspaper. Ciphers, yes, but it was a dainty little booklet of them, handmade, with watercolour flowers painted upon it. Not at all the sort of thing one would expect to find Holmes working upon. More like a lady's hobby. Holmes quite snapped at me when I tried to have a closer look at it."

It was as I had feared. Feeling a bit weak, I closed my eyes.

"Miss Meshle? I know you said you are not here to consult me as a physician, but—are you ill?"

"Just a dreadful headache, Dr. Watson."

Quite a headache indeed. The "lady's hobby" had to be *my* cipher book, created by Mum and given to me upon my fateful fourteenth birthday in order that its secret messages might tell me where her hoarded fortune was hidden. It was, indeed, my most precious memento of my mother. But my first day in London, it had been stolen from me by a cutthroat while I was unconscious, and I had thought it lost and gone forever.

Now, however, I saw what must have happened: When Inspector Lestrade of Scotland Yard had gone to arrest Cutter, he had searched the boat's cabin. He had found this flowery little booklet, incongruous enough in such a place that he had showed it to his friend Sherlock Holmes. Or perhaps the great detective had been there for the search and had seen the item in question himself.

And had recognised his mother's handwriting.

This, then, was how my brothers knew of my financial well-being. After solving the ciphers, Sherlock must have made certain inquiries or investigations at our mutual childhood home, Ferndell Hall.

At the same time, he had very likely deduced a connection with ciphers he had seen in the personal columns of the *Pall Mall Gazette* — ciphers that mentioned "chrysanthemum" and "ivy." Almost certainly he had solved them as well. He had been eaves-dropping, as it were, on the communications be-tween me and Mum.

And now he had placed his own advertisement to bait a trap for me.

"Miss Meshle." Dr Watson sounded concerned. "You do not look well at all."

After taking my pulse and inquiring what I had eaten for luncheon, the good doctor gave me a bro-mide and had me lie down on the cot in his examining-room while he consulted with his other patients. Perhaps an hour passed before he poked his head in and asked, "Any better?"

Throwing off the knitted blanket with which he had covered my fully clad person, I sat up to speak to him. "Much better, thank you, Dr. Watson." This was the truth. The hour of rest had given me time to remember my mother's face, and her habitual dic-tum—"Enola, you will do quite well on your own"—and thereby calm myself.

And reach a decision.

And formulate a plan.

For which I needed to be in position before five o'clock, and already it was past three.

Dr. Watson refused to accept a consulting-fee from me. Thanking him profusely, I departed, walking to the cab-stand at the corner.

"Baker Street," I told the cabby.

Once inside the four-wheeler, I drew the blinds. Then, while swaying along through London traffic, I removed from my personage as much of Ivy Meshle as I could. Off came my cheap straw hat, which I necessarily sacrificed, stuffing it underneath the seat of the cab. Off came the fair-but-false fringe of curls over my forehead, which I put into a pocket, and my "chignon," similarly stowed. Off came the green glass earbobs, "choker" necklace and other baubles. From my bosom, where as I have said I kept a variety of useful items, I pulled a scarf, which I tied over my now unadorned head. I closed my mantle to cover most of my dress. I did, however, leave in my cheeks and nostrils the devices that stretched them into a fuller shape.

Raising the blinds, I watched with interest, viewing my brother's lodging for the first time, as the cab trotted me past 221 Baker Street: just another numbered doorway in a common wall of shops and residences, an ordinary enough place to house such an extraordinary person as Sherlock Holmes.

But I waited until we had passed the next corner before I knocked on the ceiling to signal the cabby to stop.

Once afoot, I walked back towards number 221 on the opposite side of the street, hoping I would not have to stand in the cold for very long. Also, wondering how I could best linger without being noticed. In such freezing weather, there were fewer people about than usual, although newsboys still cried out for a living: " 'Orrible murder in Whitechapel; read all about it!" And fishmongers pushed their barrows: "Fresh 'erring, live oysters, whelks!" And all swathed in a long waterproof, a poor woman tried to sell trifles from a basket: "Oranges, boot-laces, novelties!"

I stopped to see what she had. Aside from aforementioned oranges that might better have been called "browns," and boot-laces, she offered a quantity of pen-wipers, made from the usual scraps of fabric but not in the usual squares; these were cunningly shaped like flowers and butterflies. "Clever," I remarked, fingering one. "Do you sew them yourself?"

"That I do, ma'am, although me eyes 'ave gone nearly blind by the labour of it."

She had been working by candlelight, firelight, or perhaps even out at night under a street-lamp, poor thing, for want of better illumination.

Holding a blue cotton pen-wiper shaped like a little bird, I asked, "How many have you sold?"

"Not what I'd like, ma'am." Her chapped lips quivered; indeed we both stood shivering with cold. "On the posh streets, where folk wouldn't miss a penny or two, the coppers drive me away, they do."

"So you live hereabouts?"

"No, ma'am. In Southwark, ma'am, but nobody wants 'em there."

I should think not. Southwark, on the other side of the Thames, was given over to disreputable theatres, gaming, bear-baiting, and the like.

And once the woman returned to Southwark, no one who lived on Baker Street was likely to encounter her again.

I told her, "I'll give you a guinea for the whole lot, basket and all. And I will trade you my mantle for your waterproof."

She gawked at me, but had the good sense not to ask questions. Off she went rejoicing, wearing my mantle, with a goodly sum of money in her fist, and off I went in her waterproof, carrying her basket and crying with a suitably Cockney accent, "Oranges, boot-laces, novelties!"

A good ruse, and a necessary one, for I progressed up and down that block of Baker Street for a full three quarters of an hour (and actually sold two pen-wipers!) before I saw Sherlock Holmes emerge from his lodging.

Not in a gentleman's dress, of course. On his way to capture me, or so he thought, he had disguised himself just sufficiently so that I would not notice or recognise him until it was too late. Therefore he was got up as a common labourer with a leather belt around his coat, a flannel shirt, and a cloth cap from under which his hair fell over his forehead.

Striding off towards the British Museum, he passed me without a glance. Other than letting his forelock hang, he had not done anything to his face, and with a pang in my heart I saw that his hawk-like features did, indeed, look pale and harrowed, as his friend Watson had said.

Silent, suffering a queer inward pain, I watched him walk by.

I took a long breath and let it out again.

Then I moved on.

Pausing at a greengrocer's shop, I put down my

basket and with my foot nudged it into a crate that was holding up a display of apples. Then I bought a slice of onion.

Walking towards number 221, I concealed this in my handkerchief and held it near my eyes, which promptly began to water.

Very good.

Already, at this cruel time of year, the streets lay in shadow. Doubtless my brother had chosen this hour in order to favour his scheme. Darkness would be falling when Sherlock reached the steps of the museum where —

Oh, Mum, what if I am terribly wrong? What if you're there waiting for me after all?

The onion in my handkerchief proved unnecessary. At this thought, I started crying.

CHAPTER THE TENTH

AN OLDER WOMAN IN A SIMPLE, RESPECT-able blouse and skirt answered my knock, looking startled but not appalled to find me weeping on the doorstep.

"Is—Mr. Sherlock Holmes—in?" I inquired between sobs. I had forgotten to speak in an accent ("Mister 'Olmes") befitting my appearance, but because of my tears perhaps she did not notice.

"Bless you, dear, he just went out." Wrapping a shawl around herself to speak with me, silver-haired Mrs. Hudson showed herself to be a kindly soul. I knew the landlady, of course, from Dr. Watson's writings, but remembered not to call her by name.

I lamented, "But—but I—*must* see him this evening."

"I don't know when he'll be back, miss."

"I—don't care. I am in—such trouble. I'll wait."

"But it might be hours." Shivering despite her shawl, she retreated a few steps into the house, preparing to shut the door. "Why don't you come back later?"

"I'll *wait*." Whimpering, I plopped myself down on the icy doorstep.

"Bless you, dear, you can't wait *there*. You'll freeze. Come in, come in."

As I had hoped, she led me upstairs and showed me into my brother's sitting-room.

"Goodness," I murmured, forgetting myself in my surprise at the mess; I had never ventured into a bachelor's lodgings before. I knew, of course, from Dr. Watson's writings, that there would be tobacco (in the toe of a Persian slipper, no less!) and a violin (instrument and bow laid carelessly across a chair), letters skewered by a jackknife to the mantelpiece, bullet-holes in the walls, and so forth. But I found myself ill prepared for what there was *not*. No flowers. No lace pillows. No ruffled skirts on the chairs.

To be a man, apparently, was to lack the ability to be a woman.

Mrs. Hudson tsked over the books and papers strewn everywhere. "Mr. Holmes is tidy in his dress and in his personal habits if not in his housekeeping," she excused him. "He's a real gentleman. Whatever your difficulty may be, he'll do his best to help you with it, miss, and never mind whether you can pay him or not."

Her words brought fresh tears to my eyes, for despite his trickery, I wanted to believe all goodness of my brother.

"Shall I take your wrap, miss?" She started to lift it from my shoulders.

"No!" I clutched the waterproof around me, for it concealed Ivy Meshle's too-fashionable dress. "No," I amended, "thank you. I'm cold."

"Well, miss, just have a seat, then." The sweet old soul cleared newspapers off an armchair near the hearth for me. "I'll bring you some tea." She bustled out.

No sooner had she closed the door behind me than I sprang up, crossing as noiselessly as I could to my brother's desk, impatiently blinking tears from my eyes. Through the blur I scanned a pile of papers, failing to find what I was looking for as I tossed them aside.

On the now-cleared desk top I saw only the usual lamp and writing implements.

The object of my search could have been any-where in the room, of course, but I sensed that my brother, although he might toss his violin onto a chair, would take great care of an important clue. I tried his desk drawer.

Locked.

Reaching beneath my waterproof to draw my brooch, that is to say, my dagger, I inserted its stiletto-thin blade into the keyhole and probed the mechanism therein.

I must admit I did not entirely lack experience in this art. Any enterprising child raised amongst well-secured larders and sugar-bins learns to pick locks.

With a click, this one yielded to me. Returning my dagger to its concealment as brooch, I pulled open the desk drawer.

I expected to see pen nibs, blotting paper, wooden ruler, things of that sort.

Nothing of the kind met my eye.

Instead, the drawer framed a sort of vignette of my brother's peculiar life. I glimpsed a revolver, a box of cartridges, a small bottle of some clear liquid lying on its side, a needle and syringe (such as a doc-tor might use) in an open velvet-lined case, and a dainty, framed photograph of a beautiful woman —

an object of much curiosity to me when I had time to think about it.

But I saw all these things only in memory; at the moment my attention was all for what lay atop the array.

With trembling fingers I grasped it: the precious, hand-painted, hand-lettered booklet of ciphers my mother had created for me. I wept anew, seeing it again. But there was no time for me to kiss it or hug it or anything of that sort. Already I heard Mrs. Hudson's tread upon the stairs. Clawing my waterproof aside, I thrust the cipher booklet deep into my bosom. Closing the desk drawer, I took three soft, swift strides back to my armchair and had just seated myself with waterproof wrapped around me when Mrs. Hudson entered, carrying a tray.

"Do have some tea, miss." She poured and served me that life-sustaining beverage, and then to my dismay, poured herself a "cuppa" and sat down to keep me company.

"Are you still cold, dear? Why don't you just slip that wrap back to your shoulders so you can enjoy your tea."

I shook my head, having no difficulty acting like an incoherent, nearly hysterical damsel in distress (for I *was* a bit distraught), but thinking, *This will not do.* I had perhaps overplayed my role; what if the sympathetic Mrs. Hudson planned to cosset me until my brother returned?

"Have a bit of walnut cake?" She offered a plate.

Shaking my head again, I wavered, "N-no, thank you. I, um, Mrs. . . . ." Just in time I stopped myself.

"Hudson, dear."

"Mrs. Hudson, I wonder whether . . ." One cannot feign a blush, but no need; I flushed profusely, for I really am a shy person. ". . . Nature calls," I mumbled. "Might there be . . ."

"Oh, you poor thing, of course." Sweet soul, she jumped up. "Can you wait for just a few more moments? I must go, ah, see to it."

The water closet, I knew, would be located at the farthest end of the ground floor, by the back door, for such indoor "conveniences" let in the stench of the sewer; one does not want them near the kitchen or the parlour. And Mrs. Hudson needed to inspect its condition, perfuming it and providing it with an ewer of hot water and a fresh towel, before she escorted me there.

The moment the sound of her footsteps faded down the stairs, I got to my feet, tiptoed to the door of my brother's lodgings, and silently opened it. After listening, hearing nothing to alarm me, I slipped out, leaving the door ajar behind me so as not to make an unnecessary sound by closing it. Trotting softly down the stairs, I made my escape out of the front of the house without interference, for undoubtedly Mrs. Hudson was still busy trying to oblige my very embarrassing request. Probably she heard the heavy front door close behind me. But I ran, and it was no great distance to the corner cab-stand.

The cabby looked askance at such an ill-clad fare, but I tossed him a sovereign and hopped into his four-wheeler. "The British Museum!"

Any astonishment or resistance on his part over-come by the gold coin in his hand, he promptly obeyed.

I pulled the hood of my waterproof forward as far as I could to conceal my face. Impatiently I wiped away my tears with my hands. (Somewhere I had lost my handkerchief, onion and all.) No more snivelling, I commanded myself; I was doing some-thing risky, indeed foolish, and I needed to have my wits about me.

The cab pulled up at the steps of the British Museum.

Rather than getting out, I peered from the shadows of the cab. I had no problem spying my brother Sherlock lounging against one of that venerable institution's Grecian Revival columns, puffing a cigarette, the picture of a worthless idler. Very likely some constable would soon collar him and tell him to move on. As for Mum, there was no sign of her. If by any chance the message *had* come from her—if it had been intercepted by Sherlock, rather than originating from him—if Mum *had* appeared, then obviously my brother would not be loitering where he was.

With a sigh of relief, I smiled. I had been right all along. Mum was safe in the country somewhere, and Sherlock was trying to outsmart his disgraceful younger sister. When he went home, he would find out who was smart.

The cab-driver had appeared at the door. "Miss?"

"Drive on," I told him.

All that evening by the warmth of my humble hearth-fire I cherished my reclaimed booklet of ciphers in my hands. Such bliss, to see again that familiar first page bordered with Mum's daintily hand-painted gold and russet chrysanthemums around her handwritten ALO NEK OOL NIY MSM UME HTN ASY RHC. And something new: On the page Sherlock had pencilled the solution, ENOLA LOOK IN MY CHRYSANTHEMUMS.

On the next page, decorated with windflowers, he had printed SEE WITHIN MY ANEMONES ENOLA. And so on—he had solved the cipher illustrated by the ivy on the picket fence (ENOLA LOOK IN MY BED KNOBS); indeed, he had deciphered all the messages, including some I hadn't been able to. For a page decorated with pansies: HEARTS EASE BE YOURS ENOLA SEE IN MY MIRROR. With a pang I wondered which mirror, and what my brother had found behind the mirror's backing: perhaps not just a sum of money? Perhaps a note from Mum, expressing regret, or farewell, or concern, even—

I stopped myself far short of the word *love*. Mum had more important things to do. She was a woman of character, intellect, and principle. A Suffragist, tireless in her devotion to matters concerning the rights of the fair sex. A free-thinker. And an artist.

A very good artist, as evidenced by the lovingly—or to choose another word, the exquisitely
rendered flowers adorning the booklet in my hands.

While I adored Mum's handiwork, I found myself now turning my attention to my brother's notations. He had pencilled them so lightly that I
could easily have erased them, so that my cipher
book would be once again the way Mum had
given it to me. But rather to my surprise, I found
that I wanted to keep Sherlock's intrusions. I
wanted to possess something of my brother, if only
his small, precise lettering beneath my mother's
artistic flourishes.

Handwriting tells a great deal about a person in
my opinion, both that which is plain to be seen and
that which may be hidden. I had been thinking of
my brother Sherlock as the great detective, incisive
and commanding, but his handwriting was smaller
than my mother's. He did not think of himself as so
very big. He might indeed be a bit shy in his way, as
I was.

Although severely logical. My mother's fanciful
handwriting could have been put down to artistic
temperament, but just the same, I thought, it showed
her aspirations, her idealism, her dreams. But in my

brother's printing: no dreams. His was the bleak realism of the scientist.

Although, I cautioned myself, under different circumstances—perhaps a letter to a friend, written instead of printed, would show more heart. People can have different handwritings. Look at Lady Cecily.

Perhaps not the best example. Her handwritings were *too* different. Her perfectly modest, correct, stylish notes and letters on the one hand, but then her big, childish, backwards scrawl on the other—

Hand.

And suddenly, while I lounged half-drowsing before my fire, with nary a thought of accomplishing anything or finding anyone, up flashed a memory of Lady Cecily's desk. As if my mind had slipped a slide into a magic lantern, projecting an image, I saw the lady's lovely jade writing implements. Placed to the left.

And I quite clearly remembered seeing Lily, the too-faithful maid, then shift ink-pot, pen, et cetera, over to the right.

A shock of insight jolted me wide-awake. I sat bolt upright, staring.

At my own dressing-table, its very modest hair-brush, comb, jar of hand-cream, and so forth positioned upon the right side, of course, because I am - right-handed.

But how had Lady Cecily's silver-embossed dresser set been placed?

"Oh, my *stars*," I whispered.

CHAPTER THE ELEVENTH

"HOT WATER, MISS MESHLE!"

Thus startled out of a few hours of sleep by my landlady's too-cheery bellow, I groaned aloud: My triumphant feelings in regard to my brother Sherlock had vanished overnight, replaced by terror of possible consequences.

"Miss Meshle, are you awake?" Confound the deaf old woman, she had not, of course, heard my less-than-civil response.

I felt disinclined to get up and go to work. And one would think I could have lain abed, for the terms of Miss Meshle's employment with Dr. Ragostin were exceedingly lenient—yet I could not sleep through the morning in my own lodging without exciting the curiosity of my landlady.

"Miss Meshle!" Mrs. Tupper rapped on the door.

"Ye gods!" I muttered naughtily to myself before I called aloud, "I'm awake!"

"Eh? Are you up?"

"Yes! Thank you! Mrs. Tupper!"

Of course it would be blood pudding that morning for breakfast. I loathe blood pudding. On that and other accounts, Miss Meshle reported to work in an ungracious frame of mind.

Yesterday (perhaps fortunately) there had been no time for me to think about my brother Sherlock, but now I realised the danger he presented, as he knew so much more than he should.

As evidenced in IVY MEET ME STEPS BRITISH MUSEUM, he knew my assumed name.

He knew, Doctor Watson had said, that I had money.

He knew of my enciphered communications with Mum, and had decrypted them.

And worst of all, at any moment he might learn much more from his best friend, the aforementioned Dr. Watson. Suppose my brother relented of his rudeness to Watson and confided in him? And suppose that Watson then confessed to Holmes concerning his visit to Dr. Ragostin? In the space of one simple conversation, Sherlock Holmes could have his attention quite thoroughly focused upon Ivy Meshle.

"Curses!" I muttered as I entered my office. "Curses, bosh, and humbug. Suppose crows turn white." Sitting down by the hearth, I pushed fear out of my mind if not quite out of my shivering body. Sipping tea, I read the morning newspapers, replete with all the usual shocks and horrors. An anti-vaccination mob in the East End had threatened the district nurse. Several female charity workers had been arrested in Holywell Street for giving out "pornographic" materials about "preventive checks" to childbirth. A gas explosion had violated a home in Knightsbridge, killing three servants and causing great distress to the family. It was rumoured that dock-workers were holding clandestine meetings of a subversive nature. Agriculture continued to languish due to cheap imported corn from America. Et cetera.

But there was *still* no word from Mum.

Confound everything.

It was cold, I told myself, that made me shiver. In the time it had taken me to go through the newspapers, the fire had dwindled considerably. I bundled all of them onto the grate, and in that temporary blaze of warmth—and triumph, mind over matter—I marched to my desk. Brother Sherlock could go—go to—go to the Phrenologist, and there was nothing I could do about Mum, but if I wished to call myself a perditorian, I had better get to work.

Seizing upon my sheaf of foolscap, rapidly I pencilled several small likenesses of Lady Cecily's lovely head. On one of them I sketched an elaborately trimmed wide-brimmed hat; upon another a flat "Gypsy" bonnet, on another a straw boater, on another a tiny hat supporting a spray of feathers as was the latest fashion, and on another a plain shawl. The fire died down again, and the room grew colder and colder; I shivered, my fingers stiffening so that they held the pencil with difficulty, but I kept drawing. I depicted Lady Cecily with her hair in a bun and no hat at all, then with a rag of cloth wrapped around her head, and then in a maid's cap, with a comb that stood up at the back of her head like a wren's tail, with a snood, and finally in a veil. Finished to my satisfaction, I reached for the bell-pull and rang.

"Joddy," I requested when that eager boy appeared, "would you replenish the fire, please?"

He sprang to do so. Taking a seat in the armchair,

stretching my hands towards the welcome flames, I left my sketches on the desk where he would see them as he returned from refilling the coal scuttle.

Surreptitiously I watched him from the corner of my eye. He glanced at the drawings, and then he jerked to a halt, staring, and after that it did not matter that I turned my head to watch him with interest, for his whole attention had fixed on the sketches.

I got up to stand beside him. "Do you still recognise her?" I asked.

Quite forgetting his manners, he nodded.

I let his lapse pass to ask, "When did you see her?"

"I don't rightly know, Miss Meshle."

"Last year?"

"No! This past week or two."

"On a street corner. With a basket."

"Yes."

"And what was she wearing?"

He pointed at the picture of a girl with a rag wound around her head.

"Ah," I murmured, so surprised that I forgot any further questions. Indeed, I felt rather weak.

What one wears on one's head, you see, indicates

one's station in society as surely as if one wore a placard around one's neck.

And in this case, Lady Cecily's placard would have said "desperately poor."

So much for my theory that, like me, she was attempting to minister to London's destitute.

Instead, it would seem that she had *joined* the ranks of those who live in poverty.

Several hours later, in a paisley dolman over an expensive but restrained visiting-dress of Prussian blue merino, "Mrs. Ragostin" once more approached the stately residence of Sir Eustace Alistair, Baronet.

But rather than going immediately to the door, I stood on the pavement, studying the baronet's abode. While mansions in the country tend to spread horizontally, those in crowded London are necessarily built on a vertical plan, with the kitchen in the basement, the dining-room above (served by a dumb-waiter), the drawing-room above that (away from the noise and dirt of the street), bedchambers on the next floor, and then the children's nursery and schoolroom on the next, and so on up to the servants' quarters and the attic.

Lady Cecily's bedchamber, I knew from my previous visit, was located on the children's level, just below the servants' quarters.

Studying the distance from that floor to the ground, I shook my head. Then, remembering my ladylike charade in time to restrain my usual long-legged stride, I minced around the side of the house to see whether the situation somehow looked better from the back.

It did not, of course, and while I peered at Lady Cecily's windows, several astonished servants paused in their outdoor tasks to peer at *me*.

"You!" Imperiously I beckoned to a scullion-boy struggling with slop buckets. "Come here."

He obeyed me instantly, of course, even though he had not a notion who I was, for I had assumed the manner as well as the clothing of the ruling class.

When he stood before me I asked more quietly, "The ladder by which Lady Cecily took her leave — where is it kept?" For the ladder must necessarily be on the premises. No one could carry such a thing through London at night without being noticed.

Rendered speechless by such a frank question on such a forbidden subject, the lad merely gestured towards the carriage house, which was quite large enough to have provided lodging for several families less blessed with riches than the baronet's.

In the carriage yard stood a handsome barouche which three grooms were polishing. Or had been, until my advent had shocked them motionless.

I sailed towards them. "Let me see this ladder," I commanded.

One of them, presumably he with the most presence of mind, led me into the carriage house and pointed upward to where the ladder resided upon the rafters.

A very solid wooden ladder.

In four sections.

Any one of which would have been quite heavy for me to lift, and next to impossible for me to get down from its storage place without help.

And all four of which needed to be fastened together and raised *all at once* to reach Lady Cecily's window.

"Thank you," I said, and walked away as I had walked in, without explanation. With my thoughts in the sort of yarn-basket snarl I was coming to find customary.

After pausing, breathing in a well-disciplined manner, and invoking the memory of my mother's face in order to steady myself, I approached the front door and knocked. *Be timid,* I reminded myself as the scowling butler faced me. *Dr. Ragostin's child bride, homely, bashful, and terribly naïve.*

It was quite easy at that point for me to feel myself naïve.

This time Lady Theodora awaited me at the top of the grand staircase, receiving me formally in the drawing-room, making it all the more difficult for me to communicate to her the most peculiar and irregular thoughts upon my mind. As did her dress of three fabrics: black taffeta bodice and train over a violet velvet skirt draped to show a finely pleated underskirt of grey silk. This costume, and her heavy necklace of glinting black gems, offset the pallor of her lovely face. Elaborate as her gown was, yet because of its colours I felt as if already she were in mourning, as if her daughter Lady Cecily had passed away some time ago.

With her head erect and a cold look on her white face Lady Theodora stood to greet me, but I noticed that in the few days since I had seen her last, she had grown perceptibly thinner.

Crossing the room to her, instead of any of the usual polite preliminaries I blurted, "You must not give up hope, my lady!"

For a moment she stiffened, but then her dignity crumbled like ice on a stream when the spring floods break it away. "Oh, Mrs. Ragostin!" Sagging, she reached for my hands, and we sat facing one another on a settee, nearly knee to knee. "Oh, my dear Mrs. Ragostin, I *know* I must continue to hope for the best, but how *can* I, when there has been no news at all of my daughter?" She leaned towards me even more anxiously, trembling. "Has Dr. Ragostin found any trace, any sign, any *clue* of my poor, lost Cecily?"

I answered cautiously. "There are some indications, perhaps."

"Oh!" One hand flew to her jewelled throat as she gasped for breath; for the sake of her dress she wore a "compressed waist" today. That is to say, she was tightly laced, and her wretched corset made this conversation most difficult, lest she fall down in a faint.

"Dr. Ragostin considered that once again I should be the one to interview you," I murmured, "rather than himself, for the matter is delicate."

"Yes, of course. I am all in a flutter—that is, I had begun to fear—"

"I assure you, Dr. Ragostin has looked into the case most assiduously."

"Of course."

"He has requested me to ask you something."

"Anything!" Once more she clasped both my hands.

I took a deep breath—which I was able to do, for I wore a corset only to hold my hip regulators and bust enhancer in place.

I asked, "Was Lady Cecily left-handed?"

A simple enough question, one would think. But not when addressed to a member of the aristocracy.

"Certainly not!" Lady Theodora snatched herself away from my touch. "What a—I never—a baronet's daughter, left-handed?"

Having surmised it might be like this, I had prepared myself. Reacting not at all to Lady Theodora's bristling shock, her outrage, I murmured in soothing tones, "Of course not *now*, my lady." A lie, for I believed the girl indulged her left hand in the privacy of her rooms. "But when Lady Cecily was quite small—one can hardly expect an infant to be aware of the proprieties, can one? At that time did she exhibit any tendency towards left-handedness?"

Lady Theodora's glare slid away from my meek but direct gaze. Looking at the velvety, flowered carpet, she muttered, "Perhaps her nurse might have mentioned something of the sort."

"Did her governess ever comment on it?"

"Why, I—it is difficult to recall—*if* Lady Cecily was ever at all left-handed, why, the inclination was trained out of her, of course."

This was an admission of such magnitude that it sent shivers up my spine, and not for any reason Lady Theodora could have understood. Indeed, I doubt I myself would have taken such a viewpoint if it were not for the extraordinary freedom of my own upbringing. But having been raised by a mother who believed in letting growing things alone, I was imagining how it must have been for Lady Cecily: Her baby fingers had been smacked when she tried to use the "wrong" hand, toys taken away from her left hand and placed in her right, and oh, the scoldings. Her left hand might have been tied behind her when it was time for her to learn to print her letters. All through her schooling, her knuckles must have often been rapped. Or her left palm might have been beaten with a strap.

And along with these restrictive torments, she had undergone all the usual rigours of learning to be an ornament to upper-class society. She had walked with a book on her head for perfect posture. She had learned to embroider—with her right hand—and be "well versed in all handicrafts"—with her right hand—and draw blurry little candy-coloured pastels.

But could it be that her left hand wrote large, dark thoughts in her journals? And her left hand created strong, stark charcoal drawings?

My mother had mentioned to me—it seemed so long ago, those wild and free childhood days at Ferndell Hall, but really it was less than a year ago—we had both read a new "shilling shocker," *The Strange Case of Dr. Jekyll and Mr. Hyde*, which reminded Mum of a study of the human mind recently begun in Germany, where "alienists" attempted to better understand insane people by means of concepts such as "idée fixe," "dual personality" and the like. She had demonstrated "dual personality" by folding a photographic portrait in half lengthwise, directly in the centre of the subject's face, then holding each half against a mirror so that it formed a new face subtly yet startlingly unlike the original.

Could it be that Lady Cecily was a dual personality? Could it be that the Lady Cecily who used her left hand was an entirely different person than she who used her right?

CHAPTER THE TWELFTH

I PASSED THE REMAINDER OF THE DAY IN A dismal frame of mind.

How could I have been so stupid? Somehow I had started off by thinking that Lady Cecily could and would do the same things I might do. Such as: take pity upon London's poor.

Not a valid assumption.

Or run away.

Not a valid assumption, either.

Or lift a large, heavy ladder.

Nonsense.

The ladder—my word, I was a fool! The ladder was the first thing I should have inspected, and also I should have thought far sooner of the garments I had seen in Lady Cecily's wardrobe, petite dresses that had been worn by a girl much daintier than I.

How ridiculous ever to have believed Lady Cecily could have put that ladder to the window herself. I doubted that I could have done it, no matter how badly I wanted to.

Also, I had no basis for thinking Lady Cecily wanted to.

I had no reason to assume any of her ideas or inclinations were the least bit like mine.

I had been blind.

And I called myself a perditorian? I needed to do far better. I needed to take my wayward mind in hand, so to speak. Apply stern logic. Reason this matter through.

Accordingly, as soon as I had reached the privacy of my lodgings that evening, I sat myself down with a portable desk in my lap and a candle pulled close on either side to do just that. On paper.

Very well. Regarding Lady Cecily's disappearance, what were the possibilities? I could think of only three:

She eloped
She ran away
She was kidnapped

In favour of elopement I wrote down:

Appearance of same: the ladder at the window
Secret correspondence with Alexander Finch
Secret meetings, same

Against:

No mention in journals of consuming passion, for Alexander Finch or otherwise
Use of grey sealing-wax only
Bed slept in — why?
No clothing missing from her wardrobe
Lady not found with suspect
Alexander Finch most unlikely object of lady's affection

I hesitated over that last as being subjective rather than strictly logical, but eventually let it stand so that I could move on.

She ran away: In favour of:
She felt strongly about social and reform issues, reference her journals
She maintained a double personality, charcoal versus pastel
She broke her pastels. Inference: she no longer wished to be that person
Against:
Who helped her? She could not have put the ladder to the window herself
Why use a ladder? She could have walked out the door
Why was her bed slept in?
What did she wear?

Hmm.

Still not feeling much wiser, I attempted the same reasoning process with the third possibility:

She was kidnapped. In favour of:
Ladder to window. Needed because no access otherwise
Bed slept in. Her slumber was interrupted
No dresses missing. She was taken in her nightclothes

Imagining Lady Cecily being snatched from her bed by some villain at midnight, I actually shuddered. How perfectly dreadful. And, the more I thought about it, possible; indeed, more in keeping with the facts than either of the other hypotheses. But again, there were objections:

Against:
Why did she not scream? Or why did no one hear her?

*How could she have been taken down
the ladder?
Why was she chosen as a victim, and
by whom?
Why has there been no ransom demand?*

Regarding the first objection, it could be explained away by saying that the kidnapper, or kidnappers, had rendered the lady unconscious before
she could scream, perhaps by the use of chloroform.
And regarding the ransom and the choice of victim,
it was possible—just possible—that Lady Cecily had
been taken for another, nefarious purpose on which
I preferred not to dwell; indeed, I only dimly understood this practice called "white slavery." The
idea seemed terribly far-fetched.

And best dismissed, for how, *how* could the unconscious lady have been carried down such a tall
ladder? I had heard that firemen could sling persons over one shoulder and manage a short descent
that way, but for even the strongest man to attempt
this from the fourth floor—how very risky. Fool-

hardy. Indeed, stupid. Why had he not simply taken her down the stairs instead?

But the evidence showed plainly that this had not been done. The ground-floor doors had remained barred, and the window locks had not been disturbed.

Perhaps he had lowered her from her bedchamber window with a rope and sling?

With the ladder in the way?

The other window?

Hardly, as it was placed directly over the railed-off cellar-way area and a water butt.

Regarding the back window, then, there would have to be at least two kidnappers, one of whom would have to descend and move the ladder away from the window while the other one lowered the unconscious lady, then replace it so that the other could come down. And then they would have to carry her inert form away.

Oh, how absurd. "They"? Who were "they"? And surely such elaborate goings-on would have been noticed by the constable who patrolled every few minutes in that well-to-do neighborhood.

So much for the stern application of logic; it led

one towards the most preposterous conclusions. Of the three possibilities—Lady Cecily eloped, Lady Cecily ran away, Lady Cecily was kidnapped—not one seemed any less ridiculous than the others.

Nothing made sense. I was a fool, not a perditorian.

Throwing my papers on the fire, I lunged to my feet, lifted my mattress, and pulled out my habit. Fear of being garroted again now felt preferable to feeling so inept.

That night, after Mrs. Tupper had retired to her chamber, the black-clad, heavily veiled Sister slipped out to see what she could do for London's poor.

The famous "pea-soup" fog of London was so thick this night that my own lantern seemed to float like a ghost at the end of my arm, lost in nearly palpable murk. On nights like this, or even in daytime when the air turned to yellow-brown smut-broth, cab-drivers needed to lead their horses on foot, and watermen sometimes stepped off the docks along the Thames and were drowned.

While ordinary pedestrians, even more so than

usual, fell victim to foul play. Right now a cutthroat could be standing within six feet of me and I would not see him. Or a garroter —

The thought made me shiver as the dank cold did not, shudder with memory of that fearsome force seizing me from behind, squeezing, strangling — then only blackness, until the blurred memory of some horrid man lifting my veil before I fled. Altogether dreadful, that night, the blackest of memories, as evil as the — the foul device itself, absurdly simple, a stick of malacca wood and a stay-lacing, of all things, still clinging on to me afterward —

Mentally I attempted to push the image away. This was no time to dwell on such a terror, not with the all-but-tangible shadows of London night all around me. Hearkening constantly for any hint of danger, I walked on, not searching for unfortunates tonight, but instead making for a destination; I could stand my own apprehension only just so long. But at the same time I told myself that many more Londoners died of sheer breathing than ever died of crime. It could not possibly be healthful to inhale air that made one's eyes and nostrils run black. I could bear it; I had been raised in the clean air of the country. But what of those who had been born to breathe soot, to live and die on these grimy streets? London's poor, I had noted, grew stunted and died soon.

One could hardly begrudge them their gin.

Huddling together to survive the nights, even the poorest folk could often lay hands on a bottle of gin, which they passed around in order to make their cold and wretched lot more bearable.

By day they distrusted strangers, but by night the drink loosened their tongues. This fact, I believe, explains the timing of my strange encounter.

Well laden with my usual supplies, I hurried towards the workhouse, where the poorest of the poor, destitute old women called "dosses" or "crawlers," spent their days and nights on the stone steps. By longtime custom, they were allowed this small mercy, instead of being knocked about by the police as was the lot of ordinary beggars.

Poor old things, they would be burning street sweepings if indeed they had any sort of fire at all—

Rounding the corner of the workhouse, I halted a moment, astonished. Instead of the expected shadows, I saw upon the workhouse steps a metal washtub in which a considerable blaze merrily burned. There would be no need for me to light one of my tin-and-paraffin devices tonight.

And instead of seeing shivering old women huddled together beneath the blankets I had given them, I saw them gathered around the fire, their gaunt faces grinning.

And with them, a man.

An old man as hunched and crooked as they were, his long grey hair and beard hanging down none too clean, and his shabby clothing even dirtier. Poor as poor can be. Yet somewhere he had got fuel for such a handsome fire, and the unlikely receptacle in which to carry it, and, I saw, a bottle of gin. And for some reason he had chosen to bring these things here.

Close beside him sat the most pitiful of the dosses, her half-naked body and her ringworm-infested head, along with the rest of her threadbare personage, covered by the waterproof Ivy Meshle had given her two days before.

The waterproof that had previously belonged to a woman selling pen-wipers from a basket.

"Sister!" she called as she saw me approach, her voice enlivened yet slurred by alcohol. "Sister, 'ave a toot o' gin!"

It was not necessary for me to reply, as the black-veiled Sister never spoke. Nor was it necessary for me to reject the hospitality with so much as a gesture; the dosses were accustomed to my ways. Silently I began handing out bread, et cetera, which the poor women grasped eagerly enough, but not as desperately as they might have under their usual circumstances.

". . . widowed. I did sewin' till me eyes gave out," the woman in the waterproof was gabbling to the old man, who had evidently asked her to tell him her story. As I was unable, due to my "muteness," to make any such request, I listened with greatest curiosity while pretending not to. "Then I tried peddlin' flowers in front of the theatre, you know, but when it rained, the toffs wouldn't stop to buy bookays for their ladies. I stood in the rain anyway and took to coughin', one jolly mess led to another, I got turned out of me room, and me very first night in a common lodging-house, some 'eartless devil stole me little bit o' money and all me clothes. Me boots, me dress and apron, me—well, everything except the shift I slept in was gone, and I cried to this one and that one to no avail. So it's cold an 'ungry on the streets I am, for 'ow can I find work witout any decent covering for meself? No," in answer to the man's offer of another swig of gin, "I'll 'ave no more o' that or it's falling over I'll be, even more so than customary."

Indeed, I had a few times seen the old women fall when they tried to walk, such was the extremity of their misery.

The greybeard said, "God forbid such ill fortune should ever beset me little Ivy."

Ivy?

Only the fact that I was already pretending not to listen kept me from giving myself away. Perhaps, actually, I did stiffen or startle — but in the night and the flickering firelight, I doubt anyone saw.

And the ragged, hunchbacked old man was not looking at me, anyway, but at the doss in the waterproof as he said, "Me little granddaughter, no more'n fourteen years on this cruel earth. Less'n a week ago she went out to sell pen-wipers an' such from a basket —"

My heart started to pound.

"— with the tears runnin' down 'er face, so I 'ear, from 'er misery —"

I felt the oddest wrenching sensation within my chest.

"— an' she hain't been 'eard of since."

I wanted to run away.

Therefore, knowing I must show no sign of what I was feeling, I continued to pass out foodstuffs, working my way *towards* the stranger.

Stranger?

In a sense, yes.

"She were wearin' a waterproof much like that 'un yer got on," he was saying, his accent impeccably lower-class. "Where, if yer don't mind tellin' me, did—"

Before he could complete the question, I thrust a meat pie in front of his nose.

He turned to accept it. In his very dirty face between filthy cap and filthy beard I saw keen grey eyes looking up at me. "Why, thank ye."

With greatest fervour mentally I reminded myself that he could see nothing more of me than a muffled, mantled, veiled, almost shapeless silhouette in the night.

He asked me, "Ye prowl all through these parts, Sister? Beggin' yer pardon, would yer chance to know the whereabouts o' a skinny stick o' a girl called Ivy?"

I handed him cheese to go with the meat pie.

"Tall for 'er age, she is," he continued, "but if ye

165

fed her beans, she'd look like yer rosary, she would, she's that thin."

One of the dosses told him, "The Sister uv the Streets won't answer yer. She never says nuttin'."

"I begs yer pardon." Something of his genteel courtesy sounded through his Cockney accent. "Thank ye fer the food, Sister."

In no way could he know how truly he spoke: I was indeed his sister. It was my brother Sherlock.

CHAPTER
THE
THIRTEENTH

THE NEXT MORNING IVY MESHLE, FOR THE first time since her visit to Baker Street, reported to work without fear. No longer did that worthy secretary need to fret, for Sherlock Holmes did not seek her; he was on the hunt for a poor street vendor who had worn a waterproof.

So I felt better, yet worse, for I had heard a quiver of emotion—the genuine article, I sensed, not just an actor's rendition—in my brother's voice when he had described me as a skinny girl crying with wretchedness.

Surely he realised I did not actually live in poverty? He knew I had money.

But just as surely Mrs. Hudson had told him how miserably I had been weeping when she let me in.

Confound everything. Intent only on getting my cipher book back, I hadn't realised how such news might affect him.

How, *how* could I safely reassure brother Sherlock of my well-being?

Such were my troubled musings as I entered the establishment of Dr. Leslie T. Ragostin, Scientific Perditorian.

"Good morning, m'lady!" cried the eager boy-in-buttons as he took my ulster.

"Joddy," I told him with some asperity, "have you ever considered that other employers might change your rather ridiculous name to James, or Cecil, or Algernon, just to suit themselves?"

"Um, no, m'lady! I mean no, Miss Meshle."

"Just so, Joddy. 'Miss Meshle' is how I prefer to be addressed. Please be good enough to bring me the morning newspapers, and some tea."

But I scanned the papers without pleasure, for there was still no word from Mum.

Well, surely in a day or two . . .

But I so badly wanted her to advise me about Sherlock. Without benefit of her greater wisdom, how might I take action? Send my brother a letter of reassurance? But—he was so confoundedly clever—what if he somehow traced it back to me?

Place a similar message for him in the newspaper personal columns?

But to do so, even in cipher, would be to make our family difficulties public. I could not risk damaging Sherlock's pride even worse than I had already. Moreover, surely brother Mycroft—who so far, cold kidney pie that he was, had not much troubled me or my thoughts—surely Mycroft would see such a message as well, and what sort of hornet's nest might ensue . . . I could not imagine.

I had no idea what to do.

Sitting behind my desk in a shadowed frame of mind, looking over Dr. Ragostin's meagre correspondence, I found myself doodling on the backs of papers I had set aside to discard, producing a caricature of my brother with his cloth cap and his forelock hanging down. Unaccountably, I felt slightly better. Always, when irritated or uneasy, I feel driven to draw—so, supplying myself with a sheaf of foolscap paper, I began to sketch in earnest. Sherlock again, then Mycroft, then Mum, then others. Faces, mostly. The ragged little girl who had swept a crossing for me. The dosses on the workhouse steps. Lady Theodora in her black jewellery. My mind had gone off in directions of its own. I drew the face of Alexander Finch.

And to my own surprise, I gave it quite a nasty sneer.

What ever in the world?

Sitting back, I closed my eyes and tried to recapture my visit to Ebenezer Finch & Son Emporium. Memories spoke in my mind:

"... sort of colours one would expect from
    a screaming anarchist."
"She'd been reading Das Kapital, and we
    discussed the exploitation of the masses."
"She wanted me to show her the proletariat."
"What I think is, she walked right out the front
    door and put that ladder there herself."

Had Alexander Finch's father merely been releasing choler—or had he been calling his son an anarchist?

I knew "anarchists" were blamed for dynamiting Victoria Station, attacking the offices of the *Times,* and most recently, attempting to blow up the Tower of London, but other than what I saw in the newspapers, I knew nothing of these foreign assassins, these secret societies. Were anarchists something of the Marxist sort?

Yet Alexander Finch had led me to believe that *Lady Cecily* was a Marxist?

But if so, why had she mentioned nothing of such beliefs in her private journals?

He had asserted that she had put the ladder under the window herself. But, having experienced the pleasure of her dainty acquaintance, he must have known that was simply not possible.

Lady Cecily had met Alexander Finch. Lady Cecily had corresponded with Alexander Finch. Lady Cecily had explored London with Alexander Finch. And Lady Cecily had gone missing.

Surely not entirely a coincidental series of events.

Yet the police had failed to find her through him, and they watched him constantly—

Or so he said.

How foolish of me to accept his assurance, and Lady Theodora's, that he was kept under constant scrutiny.

How much did I know, really know, about Alexander Finch?

Very little.

I arose from my desk to go talk with him again.

However, this time, it was not Ivy Meshle who sallied forth to the department store. Instead, it was Mrs. Ragostin. Or not Mrs. Ragostin, exactly, for today I wore a rich satin-and-velveteen day-dress not at all dowdy, and I would exhibit no timidity of manner. Alexander Finch had my-ladied me; very well, I'd be a lady—or at least, gentry—and I'd see how he liked that. I paid my sixpence a mile in order to arrive at Finch & Son in a cab.

A hansom cab, despite the cold, because I wanted a good view of the building's exterior.

Warmly wrapped in my long fur cloak, I did not immediately exit the cab as it drew to a halt in front of the Finch establishment. I took my time, looking: not at that glittering mercantile palace of brass, gas, and glass, the Emporium itself, but instead peering skyward, studying the building's upper storeys where the clerks lodged. Dormers. Gables. Drainpipes.

Closely approximating the dormers and gables and drainpipes of the buildings on either side.

Meanwhile, a uniformed constable, looking quite

dull, stood across the street, no doubt stationed there to watch the front door in case Alexander Finch came out.

Humph.

Exiting the cab and dismissing it, I sailed into the department store with my silk-gloved hands in my fur muff, my hat towering with ostrich feathers and my skirt regally trailing.

"I should like to speak with Master Alexander Finch," I demanded condescendingly of the first clerk I encountered.

A slight, freckled, rickety sort of young man, he visibly fumbled for words before squeaking out a reply. "Alexander Finch, ah, I am not sure he is in just now, ah, my lady."

I arched my brows in feigned ire and genuine astonishment: This hapless clerk was more afraid of young Finch than he was of *me*?

I remembered how the willowy girl at the shoe counter had fled at young Finch's command.

At that misfortunate moment it occurred to me to wonder: Why had that peculiar youth chosen to converse with me in the shoe department, while walking past, for instance, gloves?

Because he liked boots, I supposed. Especially

the lace-up sort. He enjoyed pulling the lacings tight; why, he had quite strangled—

I felt the strangest chill run through me, as my personage comprehended a moment in advance of my mind. Indeed, I suddenly felt so weak that I swayed on my feet.

"My lady?" The clerk's anxious voice seemed to reach me from a great distance.

As those other voices had sounded, so far away, that night as I had regained consciousness with a garrote still around my neck. I remembered terror, blur, fog, the nondescript man lifting my veil.

I remembered where I had seen Alexander Finch's face before.

The freckled clerk cried, "Help, somebody! She's going to faint!"

An excellent idea, as my intentions had taken quite a sudden about-face. I now fervidly wished to avoid speaking with Alexander Finch; he must not see me. And while I had never feigned a faint before, it seemed simple enough. Rolling my eyes upward as I closed them, I began to collapse towards the floor.

"Catch 'er, then!" Another male voice, rather Cockney, spoke close to my ear as the fellow grasped me under the elbow.

The rickety clerk, I think, took my other arm, and I allowed myself to sag in the hands of my supporters as they hustled me through a door somewhere off to the side of the store. "Lay 'er on the bench," said another voice, a woman's this time. " 'Oo is she?"

"Dunno. She wanted to see Master Alexander."

"Coo! Somebody ought to warn 'er."

I felt my personage being placed as directed, gently enough, considering how unyielding a wooden bench is. Someone began to unbutton my high collar. Easing my eyes open just enough to peep through my eyelashes, I saw that my Good Samaritan was a female servant of middle age. The high-backed bench faced the hearth, hiding the rest of the room from my view, but I surmised—if only from that rude item of furniture—that they had taken me to the clerks' tea-and-luncheon room.

"What did she want to see 'im for?" asked a man's voice.

"I dunno. Right wrought up, she was."

"D'ye think, wit the swag she's wearin' on 'er, she might be a shipyard boss's wife, like? Or a factory owner's? Tryin' to talk some sense into 'im about all the trouble 'ee's stirrin' up?"

"I always did say them factory 'uns are a rough lot, especially them match girls." Unbuttoning my cuffs to chafe my wrists, the servant evidently considered herself to be on equal standing with the clerks, for she spoke her mind. "Them and their so-called strike. Too mule-headed to touch chemicals, an' only workin' fourteen hours a day now—"

"It's not the match girls 'ee's fomentin' anymore, it's the dock-men and—"

"—and what they want with all that free time is beyond me, doin' whatever they like—"

"—and the carters and such."

"—spoilin' their reputations, lurin' good girls out of the domestic service, and this poor lady faintin' away for want of proper care—where's the smellin' salts, for the luvva mercy?"

"Oh! Right 'ere!"

With my eyes once more firmly lidded, I laid still as the pungent restorative was presented to my nose, disciplining myself not to respond, for I wanted to hear more. While my person and face appeared, I hoped, insensible, my mind hopped, shrieked and grabbed like a child presented with sugar-plums: Foment? Alexander Finch? Dock workers? Match girls? Strike? Hadn't Joddy mumbled something about a match and a strike?

One of the male voices was saying, "The carters is mostly bein' sensible, wot I 'ear, but the dockyards is all like a pot on the boil to strike a blow for worker's rights, wot they call it."

"She ain't comin' round." My nurse sounded worried. "Get me a scissors so's I can cut her stay-lacings."

Oh. Oh, no, she must not be permitted to see my corset. I bestirred my eyelids slightly.

"Wait a minute," said the kindly woman.

At the same time an unmistakable voice roared from somewhere close at hand, "What's going on here? Get back to your stations!"

"Yes, Mr. Finch."

"Yes, sir."

"The lady fainted, you see."

"Lady?" bellowed the elder Finch. "What lady?"

I interjected a moan, in order to deflect his attention from his clerks onto me.

"Well, send for a doctor!" he barked. "You men get back to work. You got no business loitering about when a lady's lying down."

The door slammed behind their various voices. I opened my eyes, smiled weakly at the servant, and told her I was feeling better, thank you so much, but my over-fed candy-grabbing mind snatched at "loitering." Alexander Finch had been just a bystander perhaps, who had chanced to be "loitering about" on the night I was unconscious, lying in the street?

Which was only a few days after Lady Cecily had disappeared?

When the police were supposed to be keeping a close eye on him?

Each thought made me feel queasier, more faint and ill, but I forced myself to smile, stand up, and take my leave, for matters of the utmost urgency required my attention.

CHAPTER THE FOURTEENTH

BEFORE THE SHADOWY SMOKE-CLOTTED day could darken to even more shadowy night, I returned to the vicinity of Ebenezer Finch & Son. I will spare the gentle reader a full account of the risks of detection I had run in the interval; briefly put, after changing back into Miss Meshle at Dr. Ragostin's office, I had then, at my lodging, eluded Mrs. Tupper to exit as a nun, wearing my heavily veiled habit for the sake of its total concealment of my features, even though it made me an object of curiosity. I felt the glances of passersby as I walked out of St. Pancras Station; these Londoners had not seen me before. In this reasonably prosperous area there was small need for the Sister of the Street's ministrations.

Not that I had ventured here for the sake of charity. I came empty-handed. So to speak, as my gloved fingertips beneath my mantle, folded almost as if in prayer, rested upon the concealed hilt of my dagger.

I ventured nowhere near the resplendent front of Ebenezer Finch & Son Emporium. Instead, approaching that seductive establishment from the rear, through a maze of mews where cart-horses and milk-cows were kept, I stopped in the shadow of a pigeon-cote to survey the terrain. Once again I studied the Finch building's windows, roofline, and rain-spouting with an interest which architecture had never before inspired in me; this was the first time I'd had occasion to regard a building as a structure to be climbed. As if surveying a winter tree for the best way up and/or down, with my gaze I traced different routes until I decided how *I* would do it.

Predicting, then, where in the rapidly darkening back passageways Alexander Finch would descend, I retreated once more into the concealing mews, made a circuit, then found myself a sheltering doorway in which to wait.

Before it was quite dark, as I had expected — for he needed to be able to see his way down somewhat, and he could not give himself away by carrying a light — just at nightfall here he came like a sort of monstrous caterpillar along the rooftops, creeping along shingles or tiles on his knees and elbows, keeping his head down and staying out of sight of any constable who might be standing watch in the street or at the store's back door. From time to time I lost sight of him behind chimney-stacks, but always in a brief while he reappeared. With a nimble ease that showed how often he had done this before, he swung himself across the gaps between buildings. Having reached the end of the row, he descended to the eaves, swivelled around and let himself down by the water pipe on to the wooden top of a covered water-barrel and so to the gravel of the corner chandler's delivery-drive.

I could just make out the pale mask of his face, eyeglasses and all, as he glanced around. Rather than the dandified garments in which I had seen him previously, he wore the rough dark flannel and corduroy of a day-labourer, and a cloth cap. As soon as he had made sure there was no one nearby—or so he thought—he strode off towards the street.

I let him get well ahead of me before I slipped from the shadows and followed.

This, northwest London, was a quarter not nearly so poor as the East End—no ladies of the night or water-spigots stood on the corners; folk here had their own vices and their own plumbing — but neither was it fashionable nor rich. Nondescript, like Alexander Finch's face, with streets neither crowded nor deserted, it was an area I knew only a little. I could count on the fingers of one hand the times I had been in this part of the city: to visit Dr. Watson, to burgle my brother Sherlock's lodgings, and twice to "shop" at Ebenezer Finch & Son Emporium. Four times not counting the venture of the moment. It is no wonder I rather lost my way as I followed Alexander Finch.

And on several occasions I very nearly lost *him*. It was, fortuitously, a night rather less thick than usual, but even so, darkness abounded. I had seen the electric lighting along the Thames Embankment — utterly amazing, nearly turning night to day. By comparison, the wavering flames of gas street-lamps only interrupted the night, did not vanquish it. Most of the time Alexander Finch, like the other folk on the street, remained a shadow amongst shadows; I could see him clearly only when he passed directly under a street-lamp.

So that he should not see me in like wise, I walked in the middle of the street — a venture I hope never to repeat. In daytime, it would have been dangerous; at night, and all clad in black, it was doubly so. Even with their coal-oil lamps lit, the carriage drivers could not see me to avoid running me over had I not dodged them: no simple matter, as the footing consisted of nameless, icy slop and horse muck. More than once I nearly fell, and one time I did indeed lose my footing and had to roll across the cobbles to keep myself from being trampled under the horses' iron-shod hooves. I struggled up, skirt and mantle wet and dragging, just in time to get out of the way of a great clopping Clydesdale pulling a lumber-wagon.

Indeed there were many carts and wagons now; Alexander Finch had led me into a sort of warehouse area adjacent, as nearly as I could reckon, to the great produce market, Covent Garden. Where on Earth—

But even as I wondered, he halted at a decrepit doorway over which an ill-lettered placard advertised:

BEDS SIXPENCE/NIGHT
WOMEN'S WARD EIGHTPENCE
TEA, BREAD, WASHING-WATER EXTRA

In other words, the poorest sort of doss-house, or common-lodging house, with flea-and-lice-infested cots set in rows, the sort of place where the pitiful, hairless "crawler" on the workhouse steps had lost her few remaining possessions to a thief. The sort of place that had likely given her the ringworm in exchange.

I guessed—yet could not believe what I was thinking—whom young Finch expected to find within.

But rather than knock at the door, he stepped around the corner of the slovenly building, out of sight.

Biting my lip, I stood like a black, muck-coated statue on the far side of the street, for, I admit, I simply did not know what to do. If I followed him into the narrow space between buildings, surely he would notice me. Yet if I did not follow him—

I had to.

Muttering something naughty, I strode across the street. But as I neared the doss-house, to my surprise a strange man stepped out of the shadow where Alexander Finch should have been. A man with long black hair and a spade-shaped full black beard. Only the skin around his eyes showed, starkly pallid beneath the beard, for he wore no eyeglasses, and his eyes—even though they did not look at me, I felt their force. Even in the night I saw how curiously bright, almost silver, they were. Beneath my veil my jaw dropped, my mouth gaped, and only with the most arduous mental discipline did I keep from gasping out loud.

The man was Alexander Finch. In disguise. But I would not have known him had it not been for the cloth cap, flannel shirt, corduroy jacket, and trousers he wore.

Intent on his business, he had taken no particular note of me amongst the others passing by. As he turned his back to knock on the door of the dosshouse, I slipped into the hiding place he had just quitted.

He knocked hard, impatiently, upon the door until it opened. Then, in honey-and-vinegar tones, Finch inquired, "Would my lady care to take the air?"

She did not answer, only slipped out of that dark doorway like a frightened animal—indeed, I would not have kept a dog in such a hole.

"Give me the lantern."

She carried a lantern? Apparently. I saw movement, and then Alexander Finch struck a match.

And at my first plain sight of Lady Cecily, I struggled anew to keep from crying out. I would not have known her had he not led me to her—indeed, I think her own mother might not have recognised her gaunt, pale face, her hair all in a dirty tangle beneath the cloth tied around her head, her shivering shoulders warmed only by a shawl, her skirt threadbare and tattered, her feet wrapped in rags. Only because my pencil had traced so many times those delicate features could I believe my eyes.

Lady Cecily, a beggar girl carrying a large basket.

He lit the lantern and handed it back to her. She said something, although she spoke so timidly, I could not hear the words.

"Work first," he answered aloud. "Food afterward."

Again she murmured, her eyes huge and pleading.

But this time, instead of answering, he puffed his lips in exasperation, then peered at her and darted his fingertips towards her face as if he were shaking some sort of fluid out of himself and into her. His own face had gone very still, his curiously light-coloured eyes fierce, focused, gleaming. His hands traced several sinuous passes around her head, then down over her shoulders. I would not have believed it had I not seen, but I saw: Without ever touching her, he took her utterly into his power. All hope and yearning, all her feeble life-force faded from her eyes, so that she stood like a most unlikely porcelain doll, starveling and ragged, in a sooty glass bell.

"Work first," her master repeated. "Food afterward."

Without another glance at her, the wild-haired black-bearded scoundrel walked off in the direction of Paddington Station, and she limped after him, carrying both lantern and basket, like a rag-tag tied to his elbow. He was no taller than most youths, but her head, bowed, barely reached the level of his shoulder.

Staying well behind them, but allowing myself the luxury of the pavement this time, I followed, my mind in a hullabaloo of horror, curiosity, and speculation, for I could not yet quite take in what I had seen. And all the while my entire person, indeed my very skin, tingled with urgency to do something, assist her in some way, intervene—but how? And against what, exactly?

I could not yet make sense of the circumstances. I could only watch.

At a corner opposite a public house, some rough-looking men clotted beneath a street-lamp. I saw Alexander Finch, with Lady Cecily trailing behind him like a child, stop to greet them. After handshakes all around, they set up a wooden crate of some sort, and Alexander—or the black-bearded impostor I could scarcely believe to be Alexander—got upon the improvised dais and started to speak. Keeping to the shadows, I stood too far off to hear properly, but I caught references to "capitalist oppression," "empire built upon the backs of exploited labour," "workers' rights" and so forth. Undoubtedly I was observing Finch, the "outside influence" of which the newspaper columnists spoke, in the very act of fomenting unrest in the working class, specifically the carters and dock-workers, as the clerks at the Finch Emporium had said. That they knew of the young master's nighttime activities surprised me not at all; servants and the like always know everything, although they will tell nothing, except to one another.

Ascending his speaking platform, Alexander had given Lady Cecily her orders, and now she stood at a small distance from him, beneath another gas-lamp mounted upon the wall of the corner building, rather woodenly reaching into her basket and offering each person who stopped to listen something small and white.

My word. Joddy had said he had seen her with "papers."

Pamphlets. For a labour union or some such rabble-rousing endeavour.

Already a considerable crowd of men, and a very few women, had gathered to listen to Alexander Finch's harangue. I would perhaps be not unduly noticed if I approached, just another by-passer, who happened to be a nun, on the street?

After considering for a moment, I decided to take the risk.

Trying to show neither haste nor hesitation, I walked towards Lady Cecily.

". . . the opiate of the masses!" the bearded Finch was declaiming from his—yes, I think it actually was a soap-box. "As all too plainly demonstrated in every good English aristocrat's favourite childhood hymn: 'All creatures great and small, the Lord God made them all; *the rich man in his castle, the poor man at his gate, God made them high and lowly, and ordered their estate'?* The good lord *God* is said to have decreed that three quarters of the populace shall live and labour in bone-skewing mind-stunting poverty, while a favoured few shall occupy their days by having their servants assist them in five changes of clothing?"

One could not help but admire the fervour and clarity with which he spoke. He was brilliant. I agreed with much of what he was saying. It was hard to believe the foul deeds of which I suspected him.

Yet one could speak truth and still be a villain.

And there stood Lady Cecily.

A few heads turned as I reached the edge of the crowd, but most who stood upon that corner wanted only to listen, whether in shock or in admiration. As for Finch himself, intent as he was on his oration, I hoped he did not notice the black-mantled, veiled Sister of Charity. Or even if he did, I imagined he could not at this moment devote much thought to our previous meeting, under what had been for me most unpleasant circumstances.

As for the girl with the basket, she stood as dull as the soot falling all around us, and as silent. Only when I passed directly in front of her, halfheartedly she poked a pamphlet at me.

It was necessary that the mute Sister of the Streets must speak tonight, if never again.

"Lady Cecily," I whispered to that personage as I accepted her tract.

She did not look at me.

"Lady Cecily!" I spoke softly, yet close to her ear. I am sure she must have heard.

Yet she did not respond at all, not with a blink, a breath, a glance, not even with a startled twitch.

"Twice we have assembled peaceably as is our right," the street-corner platform speaker passionately declaimed, "twice we have marched to Trafalgar Square under the silken flags of our guilds, to adjure the West End of London to remember us— and the police have beaten us back with billy-clubs. And after we withdrew bloodied and defeated, this is what one member of Parliament had to say: 'It is in bad taste for people to parade their insolent starvation in the face of the rich and trading portions of the town. They should have starved in their garrets.'"

The crowd now overflowed into the street, as far as the opposite pavement, yet amongst all those bystanders one heard not a sound except the voice of the black-haired orator. Alexander Finch's vehement silver glance passed like magnetism over and through the crowd, and to a man the listeners stood entranced. They gazed as if they were —

Finally I allowed myself to think it.

Mesmerised.

Like Lady Cecily.

CHAPTER THE FIFTEENTH

MESMERISM. THE STUFF OF MUSIC-HALL entertainments and parlour amusements.

I would not have believed it had I not seen it.

But I *had* seen him do it to Lady Cecily. However briefly, I had seen him make the magnetic passes with his hands and penetrate her with his gaze, as Mrs. Bailey amongst others had described to me. And now Lady Cecily stood before me on a street corner: listless, in rags, an automaton, forgetting her hunger in order to hand out anarchist pamphlets.

Just looking at her, I wanted to scream with frustration. Desperately I desired to help her, free her, rescue her, do something—but what?

Go fetch a police constable? But he would have no knowledge of the disappearance of Lady Cecily, and therefore no reason to detain her.

Race to tell Lady Theodora all that I knew, then let her deploy the authorities? But that would take hours, perhaps even a day, and in the meantime, what if something happened to Lady Cecily?

"Let them set their imperialist police on us," cried her captor to the street-corner crowd, "let them give us another Bloody Sunday! For next time we will colour our flags with the hue of our beaten heads! Next time we will fly red flags of revolution!" And the men tossed their ragged caps in the air, wildly shouting, cheering for their newfound messiah.

But I knew that beneath the wild black wig and false beard he was no working-class hero.

He was a sham. A rich shopkeeper's son.

And he was glorying in the power with which he swayed the crowd.

He liked to wield power, apparently.

Watching the subjugated girl, Lady Cecily, I knew I could not turn my back on her even for a moment, lest she disappear again. I *must* get her away from him. Here. Now.

But how? Un-Mesmerise her? This was done, I had heard, by performing the magnetic manoeuvres in reverse; it seemed most unlikely that I could accomplish it. Seize her and carry her off bodily? But

then *I* would be pursued as a kidnapper, for she would cry out and struggle against me. I knew she would, for while she looked as meek as a dove — standing there with downcast eyes, handing out pamphlets — tame as she seemed, I knew full well there was another side to her, not the Lady Cecily who drew smudgy pastels but the left-handed lady who drew bold, dark —

Wait a minute.

Lady Cecily — or the wan pauper girl whom I knew to be Lady Cecily — was giving out papers with her *right hand*.

And as this realisation flashed upon me, such an electric illumination of simultaneous conjecture, hypothesis, and hope burst upon my benighted mind that I am sure my eyes went as round as bull's-eye lanterns. Safely hidden by my black veil, my mouth gaped. I whispered, "Oh, my stars and *garters*!"

Oh.

Oh, if only I could do it: make contact with the left-handed lady, acting on the premise that only the proper and docile right-handed Lady Cecily had fallen under the power of the villain.

If the secret, rebellious left-handed lady lurked unfettered within this meek creature before me, I

had to communicate with her, and quickly, and in a way that would cause her to connect with me as if by telegraph wires, almost instantly.

More by instinct than by conscious thought I knew how it might be done.

Her charcoal drawings, you see, had strangely affected me. Touched some deep recognition in me. Almost as if she and I could be soul-mates.

Perhaps, just perhaps, she might similarly recognise me.

So, reaching into a pocket for pencil and paper — I always carried some with me — I opened the political pamphlet, hid the paper behind it, and standing with the gas-light to my back so that only the gaunt, listless girl in rags could see me, I drew.

Instinct, again, more than conscious thought, told me *what* to draw, how best to depict freedom as Lady Cecily had experienced it. Doing so, I sketched as rapidly and well as ever I had done in my life.

I drew a likeness of Lady Cecily, dressed in stylish modern "Turkish" bloomers, pedalling a bicycle — skimming the earth by her own power, as I too loved to do. Lady Cecily, strong and beautiful, smiling, with the wind ruffling her hair and blowing her hat-ribbons in the air.

And as my pencil flew, out of the tail of my eye I could see the right-handed pauper girl grow motionless, forgetting her assigned task of handing out political tripe. I saw her stiffen, her gaze riveted upon the drawing.

I switched the pencil to my left hand. Very clumsily I began to scrawl beneath the drawing, from right to left, in mirror writing: "Who—"

But I had gone a bit too far. She dropped her basket, and before I could complete the question her left hand shot out, snatching the pencil and paper away from me. Dull as soot no longer, she stood before me like a small and icy flame, demanding, "How dare you? What do you think you are doing? *Who are you?*"

Luckily, no one around us paid any attention, for the crowd roared agreement with Alexander Finch as he harangued, "Let them set their sabre-waving cavalry upon us, let them massacre us as they did at Peterloo, yet we will persevere!"

Lady Cecily sounded as if she quite wanted a sabre to wield upon me. "Who *are* you?"

And on the spur of that moment—oh, dear, how the cavalry metaphor does take hold—I mean, at that time of crisis, not knowing how else to calm her and answer her, I did something the Sister should never have done.

Had never done before.

I lifted my veil.

I let her see my face.

My long, plain, "Ciceronian" face.

She stared. She took a breath and let it go in a puff, as if blowing out a candle-flame. "Why," she said softly, "you're just a girl."

She continued to study me as if both puzzled and intrigued.

"You draw marvellously well," she added.

I thought of the superb charcoal artworks she had never let anyone see, and something must have shown in my face, something that made her smile.

"You're no nun," she said in a light tone as if teasing a girl-friend. "Whatever are you doing in that absurd habit?"

In my most aristocratic accent, so that she would know we were alike in class as well as in other ways, I responded, "Lady Cecily, one might also ask —"

I meant to twit her about being a baronet's daughter dressed in rags. But as I spoke her name, she froze, and let out a squeak, almost a scream, as if she had not known I knew her. As if she had not heard me call her by name before. As if she had been deaf then, but could hear me now.

Her reaction, fortunately, went unnoticed amidst the cheering of the crowd.

"Lady Cecily," I tried again, "there is no need for alarm. I wish only to befriend you. To take you somewhere warm and safe, give you supper, and get you out of those rags."

She looked down at herself, then up at me again with a wild, frightened stare, then all around her, bewildered and half panicked, as if she scarcely knew where she was.

"The company here is most unpleasant," I gently remarked. "Shall we go?" Taking her left hand—bare and blue, her poor hands, chapped with cold—I drew her a few steps away from Alexander Finch and his mob of followers.

"The working man has a right to unionise for a fair hourly pay," that street-corner orator bellowed, "and a fair working day!"

Lady Cecily stopped where she was. "No," she faltered. "No, I—I can't."

"Why not?" My tone remained soft and even, for above all I must not excite her again, must not risk drawing Finch's attention to her. And to me.

"He—my loyalty—the cause—the name of Cameron Shaw shall be written in the history of England; he will be a great man someday."

"Who?"

"Cameron Shaw!" With a glance of fervid devotion she indicated the black-haired, black-bearded rabble-rouser on his soap-box. "Do you mean to say you have never *heard* of him?"

Soothingly and also truthfully I answered, "I am most anxious to hear all about him. How did you meet him?"

"I—it was—most peculiar . . ." With her brow creased, she stood again bewildered, her eyes watering while she shivered in the cold like a lost child.

"Come," I told her, and again taking her by the hand, I led her away.

At the first corner I veered onto a different street, out of Alexander Finch's sight should he chance to turn his head. Then, breathing out, I slowed my pace so that Lady Cecily could get along more comfortably—stumbling on her half-frozen, rag-wrapped feet—but also so that I could attempt to decipher where we were and where we were going. Nothing looked familiar about any of the empty streets I scanned. I neither saw nor heard anyone else nearby; this neighbourhood seemed mostly deserted on a winter night, although anybody from a pick-pocket to Jack the Ripper himself could have lurked in the foggy, smoky shadows between the street-lamps.

Lady Cecily's teeth began to click like my rosary, such was the chill of the night and her fright. Stopping for a moment, finding in my pockets some of the strength-replenishing candies I always carried with me, I gave them to her. As she fumbled to un-wrap one and place it in her mouth, I took off my fur-lined gloves and put them onto her frigid hands. I opened my mantle and invited her to share its warmth, wrapping it around both of us, my left arm around her shoulder as if she were a little sister.

And my right hand fingering the hilt of my dagger as we moved on again.

"So tell me," I asked her once more, gently, "How did you meet this, um, Cameron Shaw?"

"I—I can barely speak of it. You'll think I'm mad."

"I promise you I will think nothing of the sort. How did it happen?"

"In a dream," she replied. "He came to me in my—in my sleep, in my mind, like a black-haired angel summoning me to be a handmaiden of his—of his crusade."

"Ah," I murmured in what I hoped was a comforting, encouraging way, although I had to exercise my strongest self-control to keep from shuddering at the image forming in my mind: the disguised villain standing over her bed as she slept, staring at her with his eerie eyes, passing his hands over her slumbering innocence to penetrate her with the vital principle of his animal magnetism, taking her into his power before she could completely awaken.

"I was chosen," said the trembling lady. "Called. Like Joan of Arc."

"Yes, I understand."

"You *do* understand, don't you?" Good; I had managed to keep my furious feelings out of my voice. All in a relieved rush Lady Cecily spoke on. "Then I awoke in the middle of the night, and there was no one in my room but the call was so strong that I got out of bed. I knew exactly what I must do.

There were humble clothes laid out waiting for me, a skirt and blouse and shawl such as a washer-woman might wear. I put them on over my night-gown. The window was open. I climbed out. I climbed—down—down . . ."

The fearsome memory halted both her words and her feet. We stood at a benighted crossroads, and I recognised nothing in any direction, not even to tell east from west or north from south.

Blindly choosing a side street, I set off again, herding her along with me, before I spoke. "Down the ladder."

"How do you know?" But without waiting for an answer she went on. "Yes, the ladder, and it was so high, and it trembled, I was terrified, but I had to do it. He—Cameron Shaw, you know—he was wait-ing for me at the bottom."

"Had you ever met him before?"

"No, never! Except in the dream. That is what makes it all so very—uncanny, you see."

So she did not recognise Alexander Finch under that false hair and fake beard.

Alexander Finch. Shopkeeper's son. I remem-bered how I had first seen him as nothing more than a nondescript youth. Dressed like a "gent," but aside from dandified clothing, a nothing. How woodenly he had stood, seemingly without spirit, as the elder Finch had ranted at him.

But now I began to understand: All that rage had not been wasted upon him. He had taken it in. A lifetime's worth.

And it had made him a person whom I should be very loath to trust.

Lady Cecily stiffened under my arm, my mantle. As suddenly as if she were a puppet and someone had pulled her strings, she halted, saying in a strange tone, "I ought to be getting back."

"Back where? Home?"

"I have no home."

"Certainly you have a home. A baronet's mansion."

"With Daddy always and forever droning about the Burden of Empire and the Progress of Man, meanwhile intending to marry me off to anything titled and wearing trousers? No. I cannot go back there."

I tightened my arm around Lady Cecily's shoulders, touched by her honesty. And by her conversation. One must realise that I had gone for the better part of a year lacking any intimate conversation with another human being, and this girl—so much like me, after all—just talking with her, I experienced great warmth of feeling for her.

"There are other possibilities," I said.

"Such as the life you have chosen, perhaps? How did you do it? Who are you? You have not yet told me your name."

And oh, I wanted to. I yearned to tell her all about myself.

My most lonely, peculiar, eccentric self.

Maybe—maybe it would not after all be necessary to return her to her life of smudged pastels and the polite, right-handed taking of tea.

Maybe she could instead live—like a sister—with me?

CHAPTER THE SIXTEENTH

I FELT MY LIPS TREMBLING AS THEY PARTED. I felt my breathing hasten. I heard myself say, "Enola. My name is Enola Holmes."

And I would have told her more. I would have told her all about myself, if it were not that, just at that moment, a voice intervened from the darkness.

"Cecily! Come here!"

The voice of her master.

Not far away.

Lost and circling, I had failed to get her well away from him. And I am sure you will think that I overspeak, gentle reader, when I say that I felt the presence of his rage like a force of nature in the night, but I tell you merest truth: His fury vibrated in the sooty shadows, palpable.

I felt Lady Cecily startle like a frightened fawn,

and cringe, and begin to shake. "I must get *back*," she whispered in terror.

"No!" Holding on to her as I wildly scanned the neighbourhood for some escape or refuge, at last I recognised a nearby street. I had visited there. I knew where I was, and which way to flee—

But she broke away from me.

"Lady Cecily, no!"

She never so much as turned her head in farewell; indeed, she seemed not to hear me. Nor did she run from me. Like a somnambulist she walked away from me—or rather, towards him. I could see him now, a blacker form in the darkness at the bottom of the street. While I stood rigid in the shadows, she shuffled towards him like a blind person, in grimed rags that might once have been white.

"Cecily!" He saw her in the street-lamp light. Although I heard no gladness in that recognition.

I heard fearsome peril.

"How dare you leave your work. Come *here*."

It appeared that he had not heard me or seen me. Yet. I pulled my veil down to conceal my face.

He stalked towards Lady Cecily; she walked to meet him. In the middle of the shadowed, deserted street she faced him, head bowed as if she were a naughty child. I heard him speak to her in tones that mocked, yet menaced.

I did not catch the words, for my attention was fully occupied with any sounds I myself might make, slipping towards them.

I saw him lower his bearded head to breathe into Lady Cecily's face. I saw her cringe.

Taking a twisted way through the deepest shadows, I crept nearer to them, quite near, without being seen.

"Listen to me. You listen, worthless chit," he was saying as I tiptoed towards him from one side, and his anger would have been fearsome enough in and of itself, but there was more; it was the Mesmerist commanding her, the magnetiser holding her helpless with his cobra stare. "You shall obey me or you will be punished. For your disobedience tonight you forfeit your supper. What have I just told you? Speak."

Like an echo of him or a ghost of herself she started to whisper, "For my disobedience—"

At that moment I charged. With a yell worthy of a street urchin I darted both hands into the Mesmerist's face and gripped hair. Savage, screeching, tugging as hard as I could, with one hand I snatched off his wig. With the other I pulled off his false beard.

Lady Cecily shrieked; had she been corseted, I believe she might have fainted. But with a great gasp she rallied, crying, "Alexander *Finch*?"

There he stood, in his own head naked even of his tinted eyeglasses, seeming unable to think what to do or say.

"Alexander *Finch*!" Lady Cecily shouted, outraged. It was as I had thought; she would bear ill usage from one whom she admired, but she could not abide being deceived. "Impostor! Fraud!" All had reversed in that moment as I stood aside, flinging the disgusting hairy objects in my hands down on the street. "How dare you play me for a fool!"

"Silence," he told her with an attempt at his former authority.

"Silence? You vile beetle, no, you *maggot*!" He did indeed rather resemble a maggot with his round pale head, his pallid eyes. "You worm, you may well wish for silence, but I will not rest until every police court in England has heard of your infamy." With a glare fit to cut him open like a razor, she turned to walk away.

But this man knew no shame. He grabbed for

her. "Don't turn your back on me. I am talking to you."

She eluded his grasp and marched off. Not running away. On frozen feet wrapped in rags, she walked at an aristocratic pace. Perhaps hers had been a dual personality once, but not anymore. No one could have mistaken her for a pauper in that moment; she sailed like a ship on the Thames, every inch a lady.

"Wench, don't you dare defy me!"

She made no reply but to keep walking.

"Proud bitch, I'm warning you." And although Alexander Finch's voice did not rise, something in his tone turned me colder than the night ever could, and raised the small hairs on the back of my neck.

Dual personality?

No, it was not Lady Cecily who had gone the way of Dr. Jekyll and Mr. Hyde.

I saw her hasten her pace slightly as she kept walking.

"No chit of a girl turns her back on me!" shouted Finch as he whipped something out of his pocket.

Something long.

Long loop of white.

Seeming to writhe like a white snake in the night.

It is one thing to suspect, or even to know in one's heart, but quite another thing actually to see. The sight stunned me out of my wits for a moment, so that I could only cry out, "No!" and leap at him to stop him.

Most ineffectually.

He quite simply clouted me with the back of his fist, sending me flying to one side, after which he paid me no further heed. Perhaps he remembered my panicked flight after our other nighttime encounter, and expected the same. Perhaps he thought no female could do anything more than scream, faint, or run away. Perhaps in his murderous rage he did not think at all.

His blow felled me to the cobblestones, where I lay with all the breath knocked out of me. Paralysed for a moment. Unable to move.

But I could see.

I saw that maddened villain spring like a beast of prey after Lady Cecily. Pouncing upon her from behind, he threw the garrote over her head and drew it tight.

Lady Cecily's face contorted. Her eyes rolled skyward. Her hands flew to her neck, clawing at the vicious unseen thing constricting, constricting to cut short her life, just as my hands had done that dreadful night when—

And in that stunned instant, gasping for breath and remembering, I learned what it meant to "see red." The night turned that hue before my eyes as wrath galvanised me so that I leapt to my feet. My dagger seemed to spring to my hand, so fiercely had I drawn it. Weapon raised, I hurtled towards the garroter.

Cruel. He has no reason to enslave her except that he likes to play with power. He had no other reason to attack me, either. To strangle me senseless, nearly to death, before—although perhaps only because of a chance interruption—he had stopped to amuse himself by having a look at my face.

"Maggot!" I cried. *"You*—sewer rat, you repulsive, creeping—" Confound my genteel upbringing, I could not think of any name foul enough to call that evil wretch as I plunged the knife into him.

Into the swollen muscle of his upper arm. Not his heart. Even such a monster I did not care to kill.

With a hoarse cry he let go of his vile murder-toy; Lady Cecily dropped to the cobblestones.

I think Alexander turned to face me, hands lifted

to fend off my blows, but indeed I scarcely know. I remember only that I stabbed him again, in the arm or shoulder, stabbed and stabbed again in a half-blind blood-hued fog of fury; I do not know how many times I struck him, or how well, or what words I ranted, or whether he tried to wrest the knife away from me, before I realised that I was stabbing at nothing but the air.

I blinked, hearing his running footsteps, and my vision cleared so that I saw him clutching himself as he fled.

Blood spotted the cobbles.

And on the cold street Lady Cecily lay crumpled amidst her rags, white and still.

Heavens have mercy, I had been saved by a high, whalebone-ribbed collar the night I was attacked — but she wore none.

She sprawled as if dead.

"Please, no," I whispered, starting to shake all over as wrath gave way to dread; my hand shook as, without conscious thought, I returned my dagger, all bloody, to its sheath in my busk. "Please," I begged the night as I knelt beside Lady Cecily, for in that moment I realised how deep the garrote had bitten into her delicate neck. And confound my hands, they trembled so badly that I could barely grasp the ugly thing, taking dreadful moments to loosen it.

Frantically I felt at her throat for breath, at her wrist for pulse. I thought I felt a flutter of some-thing—perhaps—but I quaked so that I could not tell for sure.

Help. I needed help for the lady.

And by a strange, maybe even providential chance, I knew where help was to be found.

Close at hand.

Lifting the lady's limp form in my arms, I stag-gered to my feet, blundering towards a modest office-and-residence nearby. Closed, shuttered, and locked now, of course, for the night, but I stumbled up the white stone steps to the door, leaned there, and freeing one hand, I plied the brass knocker with all my remaining strength.

I kept up my frenzied knocking until the door actually opened. Still clinging to the stricken lady, I staggered, nearly falling, into the front hallway.

I only glimpsed the very startled parlour-maid who had let me in, for my panicked gaze had fixed on the equally startled gentleman emerging from the

library with an after-dinner drink in his hand —
Dr. Watson.

I tried to say something to him, but choked on
my own words, for right beside the good doctor
walked his dinner companion and friend — my
brother — Sherlock Holmes.

CHAPTER THE SEVENTEENTH

LUCKILY IT WAS SCARCELY POSSIBLE FOR me to react with more panic than I was already revealing—in my agitation of manner, for my face remained hidden by its dense black veil.

And luckily Sherlock Holmes's attention, like Dr. Watson's, was all taken up by the limp, very possibly lifeless girl sagging against me.

"Good heavens!" Striding to me, Watson picked up Lady Cecily as if cradling a child. Nearly running, he carried her into the warm, well-lighted library.

Following, my brother asked, "Is she breathing?"

"Only just."

She was alive, then. Hearing that, suddenly I felt light-headed, indeed light of person, as if I might float, such a burden had been lifted from me.

Doctor Watson laid the lady upon a leather davenport and applied his trained fingers to her wrist. "Her pulse is weak. Brandy, Holmes!"

My brother was already striding towards the decanter, his back to me. The parlour-maid stood at some distance from me, clinging to the stairway newel as if she might faint. At that moment I could have simply turned, stepped out of the door, and slipped away into the darkness.

I knew I should. There was no reason for me to stay. Lady Cecily would be well cared for.

And there was every reason for me to leave. Dr. Watson's attention might turn towards me, or the attention of his friend might do the same; my brother might recognise me. Moreover, at any moment Lady Cecily might regain her senses and say my name, which like a fool I had told her.

Every nerve told me to flee.

Yet, instead, like an overlarge black moth drawn to a candle-flame, I ghosted into the room with the others.

With my brother.

With the girl whom I had wanted to be my friend.

And with the fatherly Dr. Watson.

Kneeling beside his patient, removing the cord from her neck, Watson exclaimed, "What sort of brute would garrote a beggar girl!" He called towards the entryway, "Rose, send for the police!"

Rose, I supposed, was the parlour-maid, who might or might not feel well enough to respond.

At Watson's elbow now with the brandy, Holmes said, "That's no beggar girl. Look at her teeth. All her life they have been well cared for."

Administering the brandy, Watson did not immediately answer.

"Look at her skin, her features. Our guest is a lady."

"If that's so, then what is she doing in such—"

My imperious brother interrupted. "There is some mystery here." Hawk-like, he turned on me where I stood just within the library door, perhaps ten feet from him. His steel-grey eyes fixed on my much-besmirched mantle, and his eyebrows shot up. "Is that *blood*?"

I suppose that, on my black clothing all draggled by the muck of the street, and in the gas-light, it was hard to tell what the wet stains were.

"Blood?" Glancing up to see what Holmes was

talking about, Dr. Watson also looked at me, then stood up quite suddenly. "Madam, are you injured?"

Actually, I *was* hurt, my face bruised and aching from Alexander Finch's blow. But I shook my veiled head to indicate the negative.

Again, I could have fled, should have fled, but some pernicious yearning kept me where I was.

Dr. Watson asked, "Why do you not speak?"

"The Sister of the Streets is a mute, I have heard," Holmes told his friend without looking at him; his grey gaze remained nailed upon me as if he might thereby pierce my veil.

"Or perhaps she is hurt and in shock," said Dr. Watson. "That *does* look like blood. Quantities of blood."

"We lack data to arrive at any conclusion," said Holmes, and he started towards me to investigate.

I whipped out my dagger.

My brother stopped where he stood, perhaps six feet from me. Everything seemed to stop in that moment as I threatened with my razor-sharp honed-steel blade. Even the ticking of the clock seemed to stop. I remember utter stillness, utter silence.

The knife's silver-coloured tip wore a red veil.

The silence stretched, then broke. Watson broke it, his voice a bit strained. "I think it's not *her* blood, Holmes."

"I would quite like to know whose," murmured the great detective. Then he spread his hands towards me in a pacific yet quelling gesture, and he started to protest, or cajole, "My dear Sister—"

His dear sister.

Those words—how oddly they affected me.

"Do not condescend to me!" I hardly recognised my own quite distinctive, aristocratic voice bursting forth, as it never should have done, from under my veil. "I am in no need of assistance. On the other hand, Lady Cecily"—with a jerk of my weapon I indicated the still-unconscious girl lying on the sofa—"daughter of Sir Eustace Alistair, requires more care than I can give her." Although she was unlikely ever to receive it—care for her alienisation of the psyche, her secret left-handed self. But if the police were on the way, there was no time to explain. I continued, "The villain who garroted her—"

His voice glassy and cracked with—with incredulity, I suppose—my brother interrupted, *"Enola?"* His face had gone as keen and white as a fine carving in marble.

"Do not speak. Listen." There was no time for melodrama; I had to finish what I was saying. "Please attend to what I am telling you. The garroter is Alexander Finch, a youth who once contrived to befriend the lady, and who has since Mesmerised and kidnapped her. He masquerades as a labour platform-trumpet named Cameron Shaw. You will find his disguise in the street, and you are likely to find *him* at some surgeon or hospital, with the marks of my knife on him."

I could only hope that Dr. Watson had taken in most of this, for my brother evidently had not. He responded in much the same way as before. "Enola?"

Having done all I could for the interests of justice, I softened my voice considerably. "My dear brother, please put your mind at ease concerning me. The day I took my cipher booklet out of your desk, did you by chance find a handkerchief belonging to me, wrapped around a slice of onion?"

I wished to convince him, you see, that my weeping had been an actor's performance. To reassure him.

But he seemed not to follow my meaning at all. He only leaned towards me, his alabaster features vibrant with barely constrained emotion. "Enola, you must be sensible. You cannot continue in this foolish fashion, alone, unguided, wayward!"

Dr. Watson, gawking, seemed about to say something—as I dreaded that he should—but a movement and a groan from Lady Cecily claimed his attention.

She would recover. With a pang my heart let go of hopes for her friendship; I had to settle for knowing she was safe now.

And hoping that she would eventually find freedom.

As I had.

"Sherlock," I told my brother earnestly and quietly, "I am doing very well on my own, thank you."

"Do you mean to tell me you are *all right*?"

"Quite so. Although," I remarked, "a bit worried about our mother, as I have not yet heard from her in response to my most recent message."

"Tell me where she is, then, and I will find her!"

Ah! He did not, after all, know everything!

I replied, "Such would not be her wish, no matter what extremity."

"And you, Enola? You insist on following her willful example? You shall come to harm!"

"My dear Sherlock," I told him almost tenderly, although I still held my dagger at the ready to keep him from approaching me, "the greatest harm I could possibly suffer would be to lose my liberty, to be forced into a conventional life of domestic duties and matrimony."

"You cannot possibly mean that. Every decent woman's calling is to take her proper place in society." He stepped towards me.

I stopped him with a gesture of my weapon. "No nearer, I warn you." In fact I could never have hurt him, but he knew me so imperfectly that he halted.

"I cannot believe a word you are saying, my dear sister," he all but begged. "Let me see your face."

It was little enough for him to ask, but I could not allow it; Dr. Watson might recognise Ivy Meshle in me. "No." In the same moment I realised it was a ploy to take my attention away from my weapon; one uses two hands to raise a veil. "No, my oh-so-clever brother, I think not." Still, my voice remained gentle; I hoped he could hear in its tone my affection for him. "I am going now. Please convey my good wishes to our brother Mycroft—"

A considerable thumping commotion sounded behind me. At once, lowering my knife to hide it in the folds of my mantle, I turned and sped out of the library, just as the parlour-maid and a constable blundered in at the front door.

"Stop her!" my brother cried, but the parlour-maid, quite excited, was tugging the constable towards where Lady Cecily lay, and before Sherlock Holmes could shout again, I had darted out of the door, running down the street.

"Stop her!" My brother's voice rang like a bugle in the night. I heard pursuit behind me, the constable's thudding footfalls and my brother's lighter, longer stride.

Like a hunted animal I leapt an iron railing and thumped down into a servants' basement area. Fleeing for my very life—loss of freedom would have killed me—I sped out the back way and so into the maze of tool-sheds, workshops, and animal pens behind the houses. As I paused inside a carriage house to catch both my breath and my wits, I heard my brother speaking with the constable; then heard the latter halt at the call box on the street corner.

Oh, how lovely. Within moments he would have every police-man in London on the lookout for me.

"Bring me a lantern," my brother's commanding voice ordered someone. "She can't have gone far."

I ran out of the other end of the carriage house and onward, blindly, my thoughts frantic, despairing: Sherlock Holmes would search every horse-stall, every cowshed, every shadow in the mews, while on the streets police patrolled; there was no place to hide.

My black mantle, my cowl and veil, my habit—they marked me, now and forevermore; I had to get rid of them.

But then what? Run home in my red flannel underpinnings?

In order to change my appearance and elude the pursuit, I needed a refuge.

But where could I go, with every man's hand turned against me?

And every woman's hand at the mercy of a man's?

As I had chosen not to accept the lot of other girls—would it always be like this? Running, hiding, dodging, disguised? Enola, alone?

I did not allow myself to answer that question, forcing myself to think instead of what to do for the moment, as I emerged onto a cobbled thoroughfare and darted across it, recognising it as somewhere I had been before—

Baker Street.

Of course.

My feet, apparently possessing more intelligence than my head, had carried me to the one place where my brother was least likely to search for me.

With energy born of new hope I sped towards number 221, then darted behind the house. In the small backyard, as I had noticed on my previous visit, stood a single tree of the obliging, knobby sort known as "London Plane." Up its excellent trunk I swarmed with no trouble at all, and after that it took only slight manoeuvering to climb onto the roof of the kitchen porch.

None too soon. As I sat, panting, two constables passed on opposite pavements of Baker Street, the one calling to the other, "Gel in a nun's gear, Sergeant says."

"Wit a knife, wot I 'ear, an' irrational," replied the other. " 'Ard to believe, but they say, dangerous."

" 'Isteria," said the other sagely. "Common afflic-tion uv 'er sex."

I wondered whether that was what Sherlock thought of me. Irrational. Hysterical.

Yes, it probably was.

After removing my boots so as to be more silent,

I padded across the roof to the window I judged must lead to my brother's chamber. Gently I tried it, and it opened quite easily; as I expected, it was not snibbed. My brother was, after all, still my mother's son, and a healthful sleeper, one who let in the fresh air at night.

Slipping inside and closing the window behind me, already I was planning how I would search his wardrobe for something else to wear—I knew he kept many disguises. He had even at times passed himself off as an old woman. A skirt, a shawl, and a hat of some sort would be all I needed.

Then I would wait, and rest, until I heard the door opening downstairs before I slipped out again the way I had come.

I knew I must never again disguise myself as the Sister of Charity.

I wondered whether it would still be safe to disguise myself as Ivy Meshle. Perhaps not. Holmes and Watson would surely discuss the night's events, and Watson might confess his visit to "Dr. Ragostin" now.

I wondered whether I would ever see Lady Cecily again.

Probably not.

The only way for me to be safe and free was to be—be what my name decreed me. Enola. Alone.

As I placed fresh fuel on the hearth-fire of 221 Baker Street, I felt all the pain of that thought, but also some solace: whether he knew it or not, and whether he liked it or not, my brother Sherlock was giving me such shelter as family might offer. He *was* giving me refuge.

STILL IN THE CHILL OF WINTER, FEBRUARY, 1889

AT DAWN, THE GREAT DETECTIVE CLIMBS the stairs to his rooms, his step uncharacteristically leaden due to the fatigue and frustration of hours spent searching for a black butterfly that had paused for a few moments almost within his grasp before disappearing into the night, gone like a spirit—but his sister is no spirit, confound everything; she is a mere skinny broomstick of a girl, unequipped with wings, and could not possibly have actually flown away from the stony face of London; wherever could she have got to? Why could he not find her?

Head and shoulders bowed under the weight of his failure, he enters his lodging and closes the door behind him.

Odd. The sitting-room is quite warm, as if someone has been keeping the fire going all night. But that cannot be.

Yet it is. Glancing towards the hearth, he sees flames leaping merrily, and finds himself suddenly fully alert, for who—what intruder has entered here?

But even as he turns up the gas to have a look about, he strongly suspects, indeed even in advance of proof he *knows*, and chagrin as keen as a stiletto blade stabs his heart; he clenches his fists to keep from cursing aloud. In the fireplace he sees a substantial amount of charred black fabric, formerly a "nun's habit," no doubt. He can expect to find some garments missing from his supply of disguises. His oh-so-clever sister has made her escape after spending the night hiding in his own rooms, the one place he had not thought to look for her.

"The *nerve* of the girl!" he whispers between teeth set edge to edge. "The impudence, the effrontery, the sheer, unmitigated *daring* of her!" But as he glares at the evidence that, once again, his sister has outsmarted him, his hands relax along with his mouth, his thin lips twitch into a smile, and he begins heartily and almost joyously to laugh.

The following appears in the personal columns of the *Pall Mall Gazette* and other periodicals:

"Attention my Chrysanthemum: the second letter of innocence, twice the sixth of defiance; also its third and fourth; the second and third of departure and twice the sixth of defiance again. You? Your Ivy."

The sender judges it safe to use this code — referring quite simply to the daisy, the thistle, and the sweet pea — because on the desk of her beloved adversary — her brother — she has seen a paper bearing puzzled notations:

??? true love

Purity

Thoughts

Innocence

Fidelity

Departure

EITOF P or A, D, or E??

How astonishing that the great detective has not broken this particular code, which to the girl seems the simplest! Yet if he *had* understood it, would he not be hot on the hunt for Gypsies, instead of lolly-gagging in London?

So she sends her message, ALL IS WELL, because she has guessed — she hopes she has guessed correctly — why she has not heard from her mother.

The establishment of Dr. Ragostin, Scientific Perditorian, is Closed Until Further Notice — that is, until "Dr. Ragostin" can decide whether it is safe to go on. She wishes she could spend her now-free time helping the destitute street-dwellers of the East End, but she knows who will be watching for her there, even in the daytime. Consequently, until her bruised face has healed and also until she can think what she will do next, she keeps to her lodgings.

She sees nothing in the newspapers of Lady Cecily, for that affair is well hushed up. Of Alexander Finch, she sees only a few lines in the criminal docket, reporting his arrest on the charge of assault with intent to murder.

But the periodicals do not remain entirely devoid of interest. Within a few days, this remarkable communication appears in the "agony columns" of the *Times,* the *Morning Post,* the *Evening Standard,* and, indeed, all the daily newspapers:

"To E.H.: Please be reasonable. Amnesty promised on our family honour; no questions asked. Please contact. S.H. & M.H."

It does not take the intended reader long to pen a reply and post it to the *Times*, et cetera. It appears the next day:

"To S.H. & M.H.: Rot. E.H."

If any decent woman's calling consisted of taking her proper place in society (husband and house, plus voice lessons and a piano in the drawing-room), then this particular woman-to-be prefers to remain indecent. Or, more accurately speaking, a disgrace to her family.

A few days afterward, she finds this interesting message in the *Pall Mall Gazette*'s personal columns: "llatdn at sdlu owu oy wen kIeni vgnig nilcato nytil edif."

The youthful recipient deciphers this easily by reading it backwards while ignoring the spacing of the "words." It affirms that her guess is correct as to why her mother did not answer her earlier plea: Mum will not, or can not, come to her rescue. Ever. Yet Mum cannot directly refuse such an appeal. Therefore, silence was the only response that eccentric old woman had been able to muster.

Until now.

Smiling ruefully, the reader hears in the printed words a voice that had often told her, as a child, much the same:

"Fidelity not a clinging vine I knew you would stand tall."

In other words, "Daughter, I knew you would do quite well on your own."

All is well?

I am a liar. All is not well. Not at all.

But, decides the girl named for solitude, it will be. Someday.

Because she will attend to it.